For my wonderful husband, Josh, who brings meaning to my life and gives me a reason to write, and for my family who shows me more love and support than I could ever deserve (particularly my mom with her unending encouragement and constant list of ways my book can touch lives). This one is for you guys.

acknowledgments

Josh, the reason I wake up every morning, the reason I write, the reason I love.

Mom, my medical advisor, emotional support, editor extraordinaire, and best friend who I couldn't have written this book without.

Gary, my guide in everything logical, who never let me have a negative thought about myself or my writing, and the provider of many, many sour candy eating contests.

Dad, the patron of my obsessive reading, the person I get my sense of humor from, and a friend I love dearly.

Maddie, my unofficial locations manager and provider of amazing books that I'd never heard of.

Jared, my wonderful big brother, protector, and the reason I'm so eccentric.

Awilda, the best sister I could ask for, my de-stressor and fellow lover of all things fuzzy and cute.

Rainey, my crazy other half who understands me when I speak in movie quotes.

Jackie, my wonderful (unofficial) editor and fellow

author whom I love dearly for never taking anything at face value.

Courtney, my fellow art connoisseur who gave me inspiration for a chronic disguiser.

Lyndsey, who put up with my constantly changing moods and let me be just as weird as I wanted.

Lindsay S, the age consultant and fellow inner child.

My new family, you are all so wonderful, and the fact that you taught me Nerts has changed the way I view controlled chaos forever.

All the YA authors whose endless blogs kept me trudging toward my goal.

one

The paper in my hand read:

Name—James
Age—16
POI—'80s dancing, girl pants, terrariums
Deadline—Two weeks before prom

As I read this boy's fact sheet, I was already mentally pulling together an outfit from my closet. I pictured my gray shirt with brightly colored cassette tape stamps all over it, black skinny jeans, and a hot pink and black zebra-print scarf. I could just slap on some neon eye shadow and I'd be good to go. Judging by the brief history given to me by James's soon-to-be former girlfriend, this job would only take a few hours, which worked out well since Nat wanted some other boy to ask her to the prom. There wasn't a question in my mind that "Nat" was the short, cool version of some otherwise outdated name. I didn't doubt that I'd be breaking the new couple up the day after prom, but that wasn't any of my business. My business was destroying the currently living relationship. I stuffed the paper into my black backpack and nodded to the retro-punk girl in front of me.

"It's going to be fifty," I said simply, checking my black cell phone for the time. If this transaction made me late for biology, I'd be doubling my price.

"Fifty!" she said incredulously. "Tori Jacobs told me you did it for her for only thirty!" I had expected this reaction, and I was prepared.

"Listen, Nat. It's three weeks until the prom. It's my busiest season of the school year, so I don't have time to haggle with you. If I take on any more clients I might be raising it to seventy, so fifty's a pretty good deal, wouldn't you say?" She nodded sullenly at me and began digging through her backpack for the money.

It has always amazed me what people will pay to avoid an awkward situation. That's where I come in. All the girls in the high school knew me and what I did to earn money, but the boys, amazingly enough, hadn't caught on yet. This was good for me because the second boys learned that my presence meant their inevitable heartbreak, my job would become that much more complicated. Of course, then I could just charge more.

Nat handed over two twenty-dollar bills and a ten grudgingly. The paper was crinkled and warm from her backpack, but money was money.

"Lovely doing business with you," I said professionally, pocketing the cash. I began walking away when Nat grabbed my arm, cutting off my escape route through the quickly-emptying hallway. I really needed to get myself some sort of office to keep my business transactions more private. Nat spun me around to face her and I gave her a look that said she was overstepping the boundaries by using physical contact.

"You sure this will work?" she asked me, her voice straddling the border between anger and desperation.

"Positive. I deliver the news, cushion the blow, and gracefully bow out. He won't even blame you when I'm through with him." This answer seemed to satisfy her, and she released my arm so that I could make my way, unencumbered, to biology. I could feel the wad of money in my pocket, and I smiled to myself, keeping my eyes straight ahead on the door just down the hallway. I'm sure that deep down somewhere I should feel bad about taking money from people for doing something they'd be better off doing themselves, but isn't that what business is all about? We'd be better off doing our own taxes but we pay people to do them for us, and I don't see mobs surrounding any CPAs' offices come April 15. Okay, so that may be a bad analogy, but I stick by what I said—everybody pays other people to do something for them that they could easily do on their own.

Biology with Mrs. Mathers was the same as it always was: terribly interesting, yet presenting me an absolute guarantee that I'd fail the test. It is always unfortunate to love something you're bad at, which is why I embrace my profession so fully. I mean, God graced me with good looks and absolutely no friends, so I made that into a business. Besides, it's hard to be friends with someone when you're taking their boyfriend on a date. Things always get way too weird when I try to combine my business and my social life, hence why it's easier to just remain friendless.

I discovered my gift in elementary school with my first, last, and only friend, Becky Brasher. She and Tommy White had been "going out" (which in elementary school means that they held hands once every few lunch periods) for a week when Becky asked me to tell him it was over. Being ten, I naturally thought this would help our friendship so I told Tommy they were not dating anymore, giving him my business motto, "It's not you, it's me," only to realize that this line was usually delivered by the actual girlfriend. Ever since then it's been apparent that my calling in life was to be the scapegoat, albeit a scapegoat that cushioned the blow by giving the quiet assurance that the boy's looks or personality have nothing to do with the breakup. But there I was, a scapegoat nonetheless.

I did my job with pride though, and after junior high, where I honed my skill into perfection, I had become a well-known practitioner of the art of the breakup. Girls had even started coming to me from different high schools, seeking my expertise in the social crunches. Sometimes to my detriment, I will admit that I can be quite difficult to track down. My mother (who I love dearly but can readily admit is a bit of a flake) seems to switch job locations steadily enough to land me in a different high school every semester or so. While this proves to be good for business, it also presents a bit of a hindrance to my clients. Though boys aren't given the opportunity to become too familiar with my presence and realize what my appearance on the scene inevitably means for their relationships, my clients (their soon-to-be ex-girlfriends) have trouble tracking me down from time to time. Thank goodness for online profiles. If the school switching gets too confusing, I can always be Googled. Anyone in high school without some sort of online tribute to themselves and their never-ending attempt to shamelessly update people on the current status of their riveting affairs ("Just got back from the mall now I think I'll check my mail, txt me if you get bored!") may as well not exist at all.

As for myself, my affairs are much less documented and much more focused on keeping my true identity secret. I have no easily identifiable profile picture, in case one of my client's ex-boyfriends should happen to stumble across my page. Just a way to contact me and arrange a business agreement to make their lives simpler. And what do I get out of all of this? Money—plain and simple. I know money isn't everything and it can't buy happiness or love, but it can buy some pretty cool stuff, including a nice, reasonably-priced college dorm and a mode of transportation, both of which are important when you're as determined as I am to go to a good school. And, as ironic as it may seem, I'm planning to go to college to learn the careful craft of marriage counseling. That's right; I'll go from trying to end relationships to trying to keep them together.

Like I said, you play what you're dealt, and the result of my pretty face and poor social status is a closet full of every different style imaginable. Let's face it. High school boys in general are not that hard to understand. And although my extensive clothing arsenal could outfit a small army, it always seems to come down to basic clothing chemistry: Math geek = plaid button-up shirt and glasses. Football quarterback = short skirt and high heels.

My mother says that in her day it was always the "surfers" versus the "low-riders." These days styles and cliques might be a bit more diverse and outside the box, but it still comes down to giving people what they want. Or at least the illusion of what it is they think they want. "Dress to impress" as the experts say. So as I left biology, I mentally prepared myself to be transformed into a cute, punky girl for the next week.

two

I was fortunate that all of my CFs (short for Cold Feets) this prom season were relatively the same. This gave my hair some time to recover from the constant color changes. Along with my good looks, I was blessed with very resilient hair, so the constant dye jobs didn't leave me bald. Length was always a tricky one to judge, though, and so I kept my hair at a neutral shoulder length, giving me the chance to make it seem short and sassy or long and wavy—whichever style the job called for. Today my hair was black, a deep black that shone blue in the sun. The constant change of my hair color and wardrobe made me almost impossible to find at school, for which I was grateful. Even with my mom continually moving me from school to school every time we switch houses, I can still have difficulty flying under the radar for the one semester I'm in a certain place. The only way people can really track me down for a job is by searching online the one thing that remains constant—my name. And even then, Amelia Marie Bedford was often changed to Amy or Lia or Arie. Like I said, everything about me changes to fit the job.

So, as luck would have it, I was quite thrilled when my four clients for the next three weeks all turned out to be the type of girls who wear bright colored plastic bows in their black hair, lots of eyeliner, and flat shoes with patterns dominating the canvas.

Before I had become the "high school heartbreaker," as my clients so lovingly call me, I was a jeans and T-shirt kind of girl, hair back in a ponytail and no makeup. Of course, this style only lasted until junior high, so no one really knew what I looked like . . . at least, what I would look like if I dressed how I would naturally. I didn't even know what that would look like, to be quite honest. I was so completely used to being whatever other people needed me to be that I hadn't really had an original fashion thought for years—not even so much as an "oh that's cute" when I looked at a magazine. I never lost any sleep over this little detail in my life though; my job was simple and straightforward, so why complain about it?

I walked into the kitchen and pulled a carton of orange juice from the fridge, pouring some into a glass. My mom looked up at me, surveyed my appearance over the top of her newspaper, and went back to reading. At first my mom didn't understand how someone as normal and socially inept as her daughter could change so completely from week to week, but eventually she just began to accept my odd profession and left me to my world.

Blasting an '80s sounding band that Nat had given me to listen to, I headed off to school. They weren't really my type, but seeing as how today I was Mari and not Amelia, I actually liked them. The band suited my hot pink scarf that hung loosely down the front of my T-shirt. My fingernails had a fresh coat of bright yellow, and I had snapped on my hot pink phone cover. It's always the little details that really make my disguises believable.

I pulled into the teeming Thousand Oaks High School

parking lot and quickly found my spot. I always parked as far away from the school as possible because no one wanted to walk, so spots were always free. Stepping out of the car and beginning the trudge to school, I replayed my mission in my head, along with the little tidbits Nat had supplied for me. She would be faking sick today to ensure that James couldn't use her as an excuse to not talk to me. In fact, I should be running into him pretty soon. I pulled out the picture Nat had attached to James's file. It was a photo of the two of them, with James holding the camera out in front to snap the picture. Both were making very unattractive faces but the features were clear enough that I'd be able to recognize him. The fact that James had shaggy black hair with a bright orange stripe running through it would also obviously help.

Sure enough, as I approached the hallway leading to the classrooms, I saw James with a handful of friends. I quickly surveyed the group to make sure none of them were any of my other targets for that week, and found, much to my advantage, that they weren't. As I approached them, heads began to turn. One boy stopped talking. Then, to see what had caused this sudden lull in conversation, the other friends (including James) turned to look at me. I pulled my confidence out of thin air as I always did and let my bright pink lips form an alluring smile. His friends stood and stared open-mouthed at me as I approached the stripy-haired boy.

"You're James, right?" I asked innocently, looking up at him through my eyelashes. He nodded dumbly but didn't say a word. "Hey do you think I can talk to you at lunch? I'm a friend of Nat's and she's not really feeling well today so I don't have a lunch buddy." I bit my lip in a nervous way, just to add to the idea that I was a lost little puppy that needed protecting. James seemed to be brought back to reality by the mention of his girlfriend's name, and he rapidly blinked sense back into his brain. I was so used to this reaction that it was almost laughable when it actually continued to happen like this. The reactions were practically straight out of some boy handling user's guide.

"Yeah, sure, that's . . . that's fine. We just sit here usually . . . on the bench." He scratched his head as if he were trying to remember if that's where they really sat. I giggled at his confusion in a sweet way, scrunching my nose up playfully.

"Sounds perfect. I'll see you at lunch," I said, turning to go with a wave over my shoulder. My free hand worked frantically to dislodge the CD I'd been listening to so that it fell out of my pink messenger bag (bought the night before as an added touch to the outfit). It hit the ground with a clatter and I turned to look over my shoulder at it. James retrieved it for me like a good boy and handed it over, glancing absentmindedly at it. His eyes suddenly grew wide.

"No way!" he exclaimed. "This is my favorite CD!" I found it amusing that this seemed like such an impossibility to him, but I kept my amusement well hidden.

"Oh, is it?" was all I said. "I just found it in some music store and thought I'd try it. They're not bad." (Word to the wise, having everything in common with a boy you like—or one you're pretending to like—is never good. Play hard to get.)

"Not bad?" he repeated, disbelief lining his words. "They're amazing!"

"I guess I just haven't gotten to that part yet," I said with a smirk. "You'll have to show me what's so good about them at lunch." And with that, I snatched the CD and walked to my first class of the day: psychology.

three

In high school, everything is carefully monitored. Or at least, it is when you have teachers who care. I was a good student (having no social life will do that to you) so my teachers usually paid attention to me. At the beginning of every new school year, I'd get one of those overly concerned teachers who would talk to the counseling office and set up an appointment for me. They always seemed to think that my constantly changing style and hair colors were signs of instability. They thought I had some tragic past that wasn't showing up in my school files, and they got worried. Though I loved that my teachers cared enough to worry, I still wished they'd just put a note in my file saying, "Amelia Marie Bedford. Age 16. Prone to change everything on a weekly basis."

Today, however, my psychology teacher Miss Tess just said, "New hair color again, Amelia?" as I walked into the room. I nodded with a thin-lipped smile and took my seat near the door. This class was arranged in a circle, rather than rows, so that everyone was equal or something to that effect. Psychology was another one of those subjects that fascinated me even if I wasn't amazing at it. Just because I get good grades doesn't mean I'm just naturally amazing at any subject. I actually have to work really hard to understand things, but I always ended up putting in enough effort to get A's.

Class went by slowly until Miss Tess (she insisted that we call her by her first name because "last names make people seem old") popped in a video about a child raised in the wild by animals. I took this opportunity to formulate my plan of attack for my other three clients, since James seemed to be pretty much in the bag. After my performance this morning, he should be wondering how he could feel attracted to another girl if he was so in love with Nat. Then he would start to wonder if he and Nat should really be together. After that I'd just work some magic and break the news to him that Nat wanted out (in much nicer terms of course) and he'd feel, suddenly, like that was probably for the best. Then came the tricky part: I'd have to agree to go on a date with him so that he could really feel like he was making a good move forward in his life. This was only difficult because right after that date, I'd disappear from the boy's radar. The disappearing wasn't so hard—the hard part was the fact that I was the one breaking their hearts rather than their deadbeat girlfriends, who were really the source of their pain. But I have accepted my lot as a scapegoat, and by the next week I would look so different that he wouldn't recognize me even if I passed him in the hallway.

After two hours of psychology we had a ten-minute break, which I usually used to get to my next class. But, as previously stated, today I was Mari, not Amelia, and so I returned to the staircase. James sat their expectantly, constantly glancing over his shoulder until he spotted me. I put on the alluring smile once more and made my way over to him. His friends whispered something to him, and they all broke out into grins. Boys could be so predictable sometimes. When I sat down, James asked me an obvious question, one that I was actually surprised he had missed upon our first meeting.

"So, um, what's your name?"

"I'm Mari," I answered with a smile.

"And you're friends with Nat?" I kept the smile in place, sensing that we were treading on delicate ground now that we were discussing reality.

"Yeah, Nat and I have been friends for a while. Hasn't she mentioned me?" He shook his head, and I instantly relaxed. We were back to nonverbal responses, which meant that my carefully practiced inflections of charming innocence had worked. I pulled out my cell phone with perfect grace and checked the time. We still had five minutes until we had to be in class but I was quickly growing bored with the conversation and showing that would mean certain death for my carefully laid out plan. So I opted for the easy way out.

"Well, I'm gonna grab something from the vending machine and head to class. I'll see you at lunch, James." I walked away, feeling that I had fulfilled my break time duty. Besides, using his name made the short conversation feel much more intimate and substantial. I rewarded myself for a job well done by grabbing a fruit snack out of the machine before retreating to English.

In English we were analyzing a book I'd already read three times. It was all about anarchy brought about by a terrible disaster, leaving children stranded on an island. There wasn't much for me to contribute to the conversation, so I pulled out my other three fact sheets and studied my upcoming projects. If I could get James out of the way without a date, I could start work on the others by tomorrow. This wasn't the ideal situation obviously since the actual date really solidified the end of the relationship, but I'd just have to work around that. The first paper read:

Name—Corey
Age—16
POI—Music, parties, fashion
Deadline—Two weeks before prom

I wasn't quite sure what it was about these girls, but apparently prom was something that reminded you just how much you wanted a date—not a boyfriend. I checked this boy's POI (points of interest) once more and sighed deeply. I always required at least three subjects in that category. The ones this girl had provided were so general that this Corey could have been any boy in the school. I glanced at the attached picture, hoping to glean some information from there, but was sorely disappointed. I'd have to call and force some more information out of this girl or I'd have to give a refund, which I've never done.

Shaking my head I pulled up the next file.

Name—David
Age—17
POI—Books, Photography, Culture
Deadline—Two weeks before prom

Culture? One of his interests was culture? What did that even mean? He liked having culture, or learning about culture, or experiencing other cultures? I considered calling this one also but figured that the other two interests were a strong enough foundation.

Finally I pulled out the third paper, which read:

Name—Taylor
Age—18
POI—Skateboarding, Shoes, Art
Deadline—One week before prom

My clients were obviously getting lazy. Shoes are not an interest. Shoes are things you put on your feet or spend too much money on. People aren't really interested in shoes. I shook my head at the challenge that faced me and put my fact sheets carefully back into my manila folder marked "work."

By lunch I was in full Mari mind-set, ready to work my magic quickly, carefully, and efficiently. I sat down on the now familiar bench and talked about music with James. Halfway through the forty-minute lunch period I decided to drop the bomb, hoping I could get out of this one without an actual date.

"So James, I have to tell you something kind of important." I bit my lip yet again, in the way that said I was worried about something, while still being cute enough to distract him from exactly what my words meant. He smiled and nodded at me, obviously allowing his mind to rest on a completely different track. "Nat and I have been hanging out a lot lately and, um . . . she's been telling me she's not sure she wants to be in a serious relationship with anyone right now . . ." I let my words trail off naturally to make it seem like I was scared to go on. He cocked his head at me, obviously not expecting what I had just said.

"Here's the bad part," I went on with a pout. "I think it's all my fault. I mean, she and I have just been having so much fun having girl time, and I think it made her realize she doesn't really want to be tied down." I let my brows come together in a line, fake worry crossing my features. "I don't see why else she'd ever break up with someone as amazing as you." I placed my hand over his with these last words and looked up at him under my eyelashes once more. He simply looked at me for a moment, and I was beginning to wonder if he was smarter than he looked. Maybe he hadn't bought my story and was about to reveal me for what I was. But, as always, the boy simply nodded, looked appropriately sad for a moment, and then lapsed back into our old conversation, claiming he wanted to take his mind off of it.

I had done it once again. I knew from experience he wasn't really sad. Instead, he was just relieved that he wouldn't have to break up with Nat because he'd discovered that she had a hot friend. He'd inevitably try to catch up with me after school to ask me out on a date, but with my tight schedule I couldn't afford the time to let him down gently, so I gave him the cushion for the blow during lunch: lots of flirt-filled conversation and a quick, promising peck on the cheek as I scurried off to my last class of the day.

four

James didn't manage to catch me after school because I faked a migraine during biology and bolted for my car fifteen minutes before the last bell rang. I unclipped the little plastic bow barrettes from my hair as I drove, fluffing it out with my hands as much as the wax in it would allow. Some fashion choices just puzzled me.

As a reward for a job well done, I stopped off at a convenience store and bought a cherry slushee, feeling that my many hours as Mari had taken the energy right out of me. Some sugar in my blood was just what I needed.

I returned home to put together my outfit for the next day. Though I still had about two weeks until most of my assignments were due, I thought it might be fun to try to knock out two in one day. It would be beating my personal record, and I always loved a challenge. This didn't mean that I could get lazy in my work. I'd still have to go on a date with at least one of them. I'd just have to figure out which one was likely to reject the idea that his girlfriend was breaking up with him. From what my clients had told me, Taylor was my boy. Corey was flaky and would most likely be happy to be out of a relationship. Taylor, on the other hand, would need some extra convincing. So I'd simply take him on a date, flirt a little, and make it look like we're getting really cozy in the restaurant when his girlfriend would conveniently walk in and think something horrible was going on. These situations always proved to be awkward, and I asked my clients not to cause too much of a scene or else the restaurant owners would start recognizing me as the girl who always comes in with a different boy and gets into fights. I always insisted to the boy that I drive my own car to the restaurant because I had some vital and terribly boring thing to do after the date. That way I'd have an easy escape when his soon-to-be ex-girlfriend confronted him.

Still, getting rid of two boys in one day would be a challenge. With versatility being the key, I scanned my closet to find the perfect outfit. It had to be different enough from "Mari" to keep James away while being "punk" enough to attract my next two victims.

I pulled out the files for Taylor and Corey once more, just to refresh my memory on exactly what I was going for. For Taylor I found a pair of shoes stuffed behind heaps of clothes in my closet. They were some expensive brand I'd never heard of that still managed to look well worn and inexpensive. The black tennis shoes had dashes of color in them in the most unexpected places, making them an instant hit with someone whose girlfriend would say "shoes" was one of his interests. For Corey I simply found some of my stylish clothes—the kind that only a stylish person would know were "stylish." To everyone else I would just look like I'd gotten dressed with either too much confidence or not enough light in my room.

With my sudden burst of efficiency, I found almost wishing that more girls were in the "breaking up" mood. If I was this on-schedule with all of my clients, I could easily double my income. These ambitious thoughts played around in my mind while I pulled my homework out of my backpack—my real homework that is, not my job-related homework, which was infinitely more fun but much less helpful when it came to getting good grades. I finished off my English and history papers in only two hours, leaving me with a few pages of assigned problems in my math book and some reading for biology. I slowly and painfully made my way through the math problems, consulting my calculator and the answers in the back of the book regularly. If my teacher didn't require that I show my work, I could have just copied the answers from the back, though I'm sure that would have been morally wrong somehow.

The two hours it took me to do my English and history proved to be a blessing compared to the time it was taking me to get through math, though with my completely empty social calendar, the only other thing I'd be doing if I didn't have homework was painting. Painting was the only real "me" thing that I had. When you live a life that revolves around being other people, it's rare to find something that's unique to you. Painting was that thing. The odd thing about my love of painting, though, was that I couldn't draw a decent picture if my life depended on it, and yet, I could paint pretty well. I'd always thought that the two skills went hand in hand, so maybe I was just some mutation to that rule.

Forcing myself to ignore my sudden longing to paint, I muscled through the rest of my math problems and quickly read about photosynthesis in my biology book. Mrs. Mathers had painted a rather amusing mental picture about the process by saying that if we were like plants, then at random intervals during the school day everyone would go outside, take off all their clothes, and just lay around drinking up the sunlight. Wouldn't that make lunch period more interesting?

My biology teacher always had a way of putting things into terms we could understand. That's probably why I loved her class so much, even if I was terrible at science. She also had a tendency to pull out her old acoustic guitar and teach us songs to help us remember formulas and scientific processes. As ridiculous as this idea seemed to me at first, I had to admit it worked like a charm every time. This meant, of course, that I spent many of my science tests humming to myself, much to the annoyance of everyone around me.

I didn't have any psychology homework that night because Miss Tess didn't believe in homework. She said that learning should be done at school and home was for enjoying life. I would pay big money for all of my teachers to have that particular mind-set. With my load of homework finished after just a few short hours, I had some time on my hands until dinner. I decided to pull out David's file to see if there was any way to work him into my plan for tomorrow as well, but quickly thought better of it and just resorted to looking his POIs over. He didn't seem like he'd be a particularly difficult target. Aside from his rather cryptic interest in "culture," I could probably just whip out my Nikon and woo him by lunch. He'd have to wait a few days though while I worked my magic on the other two boys.

I settled on the decision to simply finish the other two off by tomorrow and quickly check David out from afar, simply to secure my prey before moving in for the kill the day after tomorrow. Placing the papers gently back into their manila folder, I pulled out my sleek (now pink) cell phone and popped off the cover, opting for the yellow one for tomorrow. I quickly dialed the number on James's file to let Nat know I had done the job quickly and efficiently. If I didn't call, I'd have a curious and possibly angry customer on my hands.

"Hello?" answered a tentatively cautious voice.

"Hey Nat, it's Amelia," I said, wondering why she sounded so worried. There was a deep exhale on the other end, possibly one of relief, though with an exhale you can never tell.

"Good. I didn't recognize the number so I thought maybe James was calling me from a friend's phone so I'd pick up." The news that she hadn't programmed my number into her phone hurt a little, but I was over it in two seconds flat. Her lack of confidence in my abilities was also a bit disappointing, but that's something I'm used to.

"Nope, but on the subject of James, I just wanted to let you know I got the job done." I kept my tone professional and even, trying to keep the pride at my own abilities internalized.

"Really?" she asked, her voice still lined with disbelief. I never understood why people found it so hard to believe that I had dealt with their problems so easily. Just because they blew the whole situation out of proportion didn't mean that breaking up with someone was actually that hard to do.

"Really," I answered, my tone now leaning toward annoyance. "So yeah, you should be fine for prom." There was an "mmhmmm" sound on the other end of the line, which I took to mean "thanks." I went on. "All right, well, I'll talk to you after prom when you're ready to break up with the next one," I said, hanging up the phone quickly and not feeling one shred of remorse about my less-than-professional adieu. I allowed myself ten seconds to glare at the wall and feel sorry for myself and then quickly pulled myself back together and walked down stairs.

My mom wasn't home from work yet and my dad hadn't been home from work in ten years—at least, that was how I liked to think about it. One day he left for work and the next day all of his stuff was out of the house and I haven't seen him since. He moved away to Florida or New York or wherever it is middle-aged men go when they have a mid-life crisis. His absence never really bothered me though. Some kids grow up in a house where their grandparents live with them or they have to take off their shoes before stepping on the carpet. I grew up in a house with just me and my mom. It worked out nicely though, because my mom was almost never home and I liked being alone most of the time.

I had just opened up the fridge to see if there was some sort of fruit I could snack on before dinner when I spotted a note held to the door with a smiley face magnet.

"Dinner with a client tonight. Fend for Yourself."

"Fend for Yourself" nights were typical in our household. Normally that meant I'd be reheating old pasta or chicken, but tonight I felt like doing something. I always got a bit weepy and self-deprecating right before prom. It was just one of those inevitable facts of life that I lived with. With my loner self-awareness in full throttle, I looked in the newspaper to see what movies were playing. There was a comic-book-turned-movie that had been getting good reviews, so I decided that would work perfectly for tonight. I figured I could just grab some popcorn and call that dinner. Though I didn't have many opinions, hobbies, or interests to call my own, comic book things did bring me right back to my childhood—the childhood I had before I became someone who lived only to be what other people wanted. Therefore, this movie would make me feel much better about my total lack of identity. Or at least that's what I was hoping.

five

The movie turned out to be completely depressing and dark, but it did manage to take me out of the normal world for a while, so I couldn't have cared less how dark it was. I must admit though, I woke up the next morning seriously considering wearing a cape to school. As usual, however, work called me back to reality, and I pulled on tight black pants, a shredded and worn-down stylized black shirt, and some mesh fingerless gloves. I curled my hair and pinned it up so that some of the ringlets escaped in a stylish frenzy.

Today I opted for dark red lipstick, the kind you find in classic old black and white movies, where you think their lips are actually black. I was relatively mild with my make-up, only doing mascara, eyeliner, and a thin line of white eye shadow just above the black liner. The shoes tied the whole outfit together and with ten minutes to spare before I had to take off, I was ready.

Searching through the fridge for breakfast this morning proved to be fruitless. Normally I would just eat the leftovers from whatever we had for dinner the night before, but today it looked like my options were some questionably old mashed potatoes or chocolate soymilk that had expired nearly a week ago. I chose the soymilk.

My soundtrack for the day consisted of a band I'd never heard of playing music I couldn't even place into a specific musical category. It was given to me by Corey's girlfriend and, even though it made me feel a bit lazy, I decided to just pull the same trick I'd used on James only yesterday. When I arrived at school, I placed the CD into my oversized black leather purse that would be acting as a backpack today. I pulled out my files once more as I walked, reviewing my plan of attack. I'd try to bump into, woo, and set up a date with Taylor before the bell rang for our first class, and I'd meet Corey at the break so I could finish the job at lunch. Piece of cake.

Taylor was pretty easy to find. He was the only boy in his group staring at my shoes instead of my face. I silently congratulated myself on finding such amazing shoes to snag him with, and then went on with my usual business. I told him his girlfriend, Heather, was sick, and that I needed some-one to sit with before school started. No one ever seemed to question this explanation and I was just waiting for the day when someone would say "What, you can't sit by yourself?" or "If you're so cool, why don't you have any friends other than my girlfriend?" Luckily for me, the intelligence level of most of the people at my school is equal to that of a sheep in the sense that I could tell them something and they would all believe it and follow that explanation right off a cliff—if everyone else followed it too, of course.

Taylor and I talked about shoes, and then we talked some more about shoes, and then just for a change of pace, we talked about shoes. Heather wasn't kidding—this guy really liked his shoes. Even though I figured it was a long shot that someone could actually be that interested in something so trivial, I had done as much research as I could on the topic after my movie the night before, so I was well prepared for this conversation. Taylor was obviously pleased by my vast shoe knowledge, and so I decided that while he was still enamored with me I should set up a date for tonight before he could realize he still had a girlfriend. I didn't call it a date when I suggested it, of course; that would possibly cause him to realize he had to break up with his girlfriend when I was supposed to ensure that it happened the other way around. Instead I casually said something like: "I'm going out tonight at about eight to that little coffee shop near the library. If you happened to be there, I wouldn't complain." He seemed to pick up on the hint pretty fast and gave me an excited smile and nod of his head. I felt like things were going pretty smoothly which was why his next words startled me so much.

"So, who are you going with to prom?" he asked.

My mouth actually dropped open in shock. I had endured lots of pathetic attempts at securing my phone number, but prom? In high school that was a pretty big thing, not that I'd really know since I'd never been, but from what I'd heard and simply judging by my clients' behavior around this time of year, I had good reason to be shocked. I gathered my thoughts quickly and strung together a barely coherent answer.

"Well, I'm actually . . . um . . . maybe going with some-one . . . a friend," I said after a long and awkward silence in which Taylor stared at my shoes, more out of fascination for them than by embarrassment at the look on my face. I hoped springing this news on him wouldn't hurt his desire to meet me at the coffee shop that night.

"Who?" he asked me, finally meeting my eyes. That was a good question—I had no idea. I didn't even have a brother or a male cousin I could pay to take me. I hadn't ever been to a dance.

"David," I finally blurted out, quickly recalling one of the names on my fact sheet.

"David who?" he persisted. I had to hand it to the boy— he really didn't give up without a fight. It was no wonder Heather wouldn't just break up with him herself.

"I don't know his last name," I admitted lamely. "We just sort of met. He's my friend's friend and neither of us had someone to go with so we thought we'd go as friends. So I can't really back out . . . for my friend's sake . . . I don't know much about him, but he likes photography and books and culture." I was rambling off everything listed on my fact sheet for David and looking like a complete idiot while doing it. If I didn't regain my cool and composed façade quickly, I might actually fail a job for the first time. Taking a deep breath, I rearranged my facial expression to one of composure. Taylor was just staring at me with that look that cool boys give to nerdy girls who have just confessed their love for them. I'd seen it many times but no one had ever given it to me. Just for this I decided I would have to pull out all the stops.

I let a little sideways smile creep onto my face as if there were some joke on Taylor that he wasn't in on. "I'm kidding," I said finally in a way that said, "Weren't you cool enough to understand that?" This seemed to appease his wonder at my sudden fall from coolness. "I'll call you later tonight and we'll talk about it," I lied smoothly. Then I got up from my spot beside him right as the bell rang and walked as quickly as I could to class without full-on sprinting.

Even though I had managed to secure the date in the allotted time I'd given myself, I couldn't help but feel slightly shaken by my horrible performance. I had never lost my cool during a job before. I tried to blame it on my pre-prom depression and sat quietly through history, which wasn't difficult to do since the teacher had a tendency to lecture at us while the class slept. I confidently told myself that it was a one-time occurrence and I wouldn't let myself be thrown like that again.

That's probably why, in the weeks to come, I didn't expect the changes that came hurtling toward me.

SIX

At the break I made my way over to where I had been told Corey would be. I quickly re-fluffed my hair and re-applied my dark red lipstick, making sure I looked as hip and fashionable as the girl who had hired me to eighty-six her boyfriend.

He turned out to be a slightly dimwitted boy, much to my pleasure. He knew more about clothing and fashion than I ever wanted to think about, and had absolutely no trouble believing I was interested in him. Just to test my own limits, I tried dropping the bomb on him during the break. I wanted to see if a ten minute meet, mingle, and break could actually be done.

It turned out that he had been hoping to ask someone else to the prom, which he told me without any reservations, so he welcomed the news of his relationship's untimely death with great enthusiasm. He thanked me for making his job easier and I was done before the bell even rang for my sign language class. I almost felt like I could have gotten money out of him for the break up as well.

After breaking up with people for so long, I've come to realize two things: most of the time it's not nearly as hard as people think, and half of the time the other person wants out just as badly, or they're willing to pretend they want out to save their own reputation. Either way, both of these facts mean that breakups aren't that difficult, and I'm being paid to do a really easy job. But it's like I've said before: I have no problem helping people out and getting financial compensation for my efforts. After all, even if it's not an emotionally distressing thing for me to do, it's still time-consuming and that directly impacts my wallet and my social life, which is why I fully deserve the money I get.

Because American Sign Language was a class I actually had to pay attention in, I didn't have much time to plot my next attack. I figured David could wait until tomorrow anyway. Besides, if I finished all of my clients up too early and didn't find any others to fill my time with, I'd have some pretty boring lunch periods for the next three weeks. After class I grabbed a slice of pepperoni pizza and a soda from the lunch line and headed for a little hallway right outside the library. There weren't usually many people there, so I didn't run the risk of running into a client or one of their ex-boyfriends. As I sat and quietly finished off my lunch, it dawned on me that instead of just trying to beat my old records of jobs finished in a week, I might as well blast the record right out of the water. So what if I didn't have anything to do during lunch for the next few weeks? People always ended up coming to me for a job, so beating my record was just my way of freeing up some time so that I could take a few extra clients on.

I threw away the remnants of my now half-eaten and cold pizza and reviewed David's file one more time. The picture on the file struck me as odd. Claire, short for Clarice, who had given me the file, was like all of the other cool punk girls I had been dealing with that week, but the boy staring up at me in the picture didn't look anything like James or Corey or Taylor. This boy had shaggy dirty blond hair, bright green eyes, and a light blue shirt on. He looked like a mix between a preppy class president and a poetic boy you'd find skulking around a coffee shop. It just didn't fit with what I had come to expect from these girls.

Trying to put this unsettling fact behind me, I made my way through the busy school filled with hormones and greasy food to find David. I couldn't do much about breaking up with him today since Claire wasn't supposed to be "sick" until tomorrow, so I simply observed from a distance.

There he sat, his hand lazily entwined with Claire's, the two of them sitting next to each other and surrounded by their single friends. It was a typical scene; Claire talked animatedly with her friends, hardly acknowledging David's presence, as if he were an accessory in her life who was only there until she decided to stop putting up with him tomorrow. The only unusual thing about this scene was that David looked just as bored. Rather than trying to joke with his friends to impress Claire or constantly attempting to get her attention, he looked around his small clique repeatedly, as if searching the crowd for someone. As he looked over the shoulder of a little blonde girl, our eyes met for a second. In a moment of panic, I quickly ducked behind the closest object I could find, which happened to be a senior on the football team. The jock looked down at me with mild interest, and then continued walking, destroying my shelter.

When I straightened back up, however, David was no longer looking at me but had his eyes trained on the floor with an amused smile playing across his lips. This behavior was slightly distressing, but I attributed it, once more, to my pre-prom melancholy. For the rest of the lunch period, I sat a good distance from Claire and David, peeking over the top of the school newspaper at the "happy couple" to see if I needed to change my plan of attack. I mean, this boy certainly didn't look like the type who would be into black skinny jeans and over-processed hair, but sometimes opposites really do attract. And he did seem to like Claire . . . a little. Either way, my chances of finishing the break up tomorrow looked good because either he was into those kinds of girls or he wasn't interested in Claire to begin with. It appeared my job would be that much simpler.

I left my little makeshift hiding spot right before the bell rang so that I wouldn't accidentally bump into either of them, and made my way to math, my last—and worst—class of the day.

The house was empty when I got home from school, which wasn't unusual, so I went upstairs and did my homework, which also wasn't unusual. My life was pretty well compartmentalized. I went to school, I worked, I came home, I did my homework, I ate, I went to bed. That was my life in a nutshell. The occasional movie night with myself was there so I wouldn't slip into complete routine nonexistence.

After I finished my homework I decided to call Claire, just to straighten things up and put my mind at ease for tomorrow. Claire was one of my regulars—I assisted her at least twice a month in her breakups even when I had to do it from a different high school—so she was one of the five numbers I actually had programmed into my phone. The other numbers were my own house, my mom's cell, my mom's work, and the paint supply store down the street.

"Hey, Amelia. We're still on for tomorrow, right?" Claire asked instead of the traditional "hello." It felt nice to actually have someone my own age know it was me when they picked up the phone. Claire and I were almost friends, except that we weren't, because she was my client and the only time we talked was when it was business. But it still almost felt like I had a friend.

"Yeah we're still on for tomorrow but I have a quick question." I didn't quite know how to say, "Your boyfriend doesn't look as weird as you. Are you sure I should dress like you?" So I just settled for, "I came to check on David today during lunch and he looks a bit . . . reserved." That was a nice way to put it. "Are you sure I should go for the whole edgy and cool look tomorrow?" I thought it was a fair enough question and I had helped Claire out enough times that she should be able to trust that my concerns were legitimate. I heard a high-pitched giggle on the other end of the phone, but I wasn't quite sure what to make of it.

"Trust me, David loves girls like me," Claire assured me. "He just likes to dress like a stuffed-shirt for some unknown reason." Claire was the one dating him, so I assumed she knew what she was talking about and made a noncommittal humming noise on my end of the phone as an answer to that statement.

"Was there anything else?" she asked, now becoming slightly impatient.

"Yeah, just one thing. You wrote on his interests that he likes culture? What exactly does that mean?" Claire was a smart enough girl, but sometimes she needed a push in the "understandable" direction. It's like most things made sense to her, but she just couldn't understand why other people didn't understand what she meant when she would suddenly say "dancing hippos" during a phone conversation.

"Culture. You know, like why people do what they do and stuff."

"Like psychology? Or anthropology? Sociology?" I asked, hoping she would just explain herself so I wouldn't have to pry more information out of her using words she probably didn't know.

"Yeah, like that," she said after a long and thoughtful pause. Or at least, I assumed it was a thoughtful pause.

"Got it. That's all I needed to know. Thanks, Claire. And I should have it done by tomorrow, so you'd better start developing a fever before school." She giggled at this statement and then hung up the phone without a good-bye. She was always kind of off in her own world. The normal social rules like greetings and good-byes didn't really apply to her. Claire just sort of flitted around life, dating every boy she saw and giggling at things that were never really meant to be taken as jokes. I shrugged at this unusual end to the conversation and began dialing the number for my other client to let her know Corey had been taken care of and she was free to pursue her potential prom date.

The note I found on the fridge last night was there again but the date was scribbled out with the current one written right underneath it. I had been noticing that my mom had been having more and more "client dinners" lately. I was starting to think that maybe this was code for "my mom is going on dates but doesn't want to bring a man back to the house because she just never knows what her daughter will look like from day to day." I could accept this. It was a reasonable enough fear. But I was slightly upset that she didn't think she could trust me enough to tell me that she was dating at all. I glared at the note for a moment before returning to my room and pulling a new outfit out for my "date" that night. I had some black leggings that almost looked like they were plastic. They grew tight at the ankles where a short zipper went from my anklebone to my mid-calf. I figured these pants were good for attracting the eye to my feet, where my expensive black heels now resided. They were strappy and edgy and exactly what I needed to snag Taylor. I finished the look off with an oversized white T-shirt that hung off one of my shoulders, showing enough collarbone to be alluring without being trashy.

Once I finally arrived at the coffee shop I ordered a raspberry hot chocolate, not really feeling in the mood to be injected with caffeine and over-priced coffee. I found a comfy love seat in a small secluded area of the coffee shop and watched the door like a hawk, hoping Taylor would get here quickly so I could get this over with and spend some quality painting time in my room that night. After about ten minutes I actually started to worry that I had overestimated my charm. Maybe he really didn't want to come and meet me at the coffee shop. Maybe my shoes weren't enough to attract him. Or maybe I had really slipped up when I told him I was going to prom with someone else, and he didn't believe my pathetic attempt at reassuring him that it was a joke.

All of these thoughts swam around in my head, making me more and more panicked by the second. Now my gaze on the door became more intense, as if I could will him to walk through it if I stared at it long enough. Just as I was about to get up and admit defeat, Taylor walked in, looking as if he had spent way too much time trying to do his hair in a stylish way. I quickly regained my composure and tried to look interested in the magazine I had placed on my lap. I hoped that he hadn't noticed me staring at the door like a maniac when he walked in, but he seemed unfazed which I took as a good sign.

"Sorry I'm late," he said in his "cool boy" voice that told me he wasn't really sorry.

"Are you late?" I asked nonchalantly, acting as if I had

been so enthralled by the magazine in front of me that his presence hadn't even fazed me. He looked worried for a moment by my less-than-enthusiastic reaction but quickly hid his disappointment and sat next to me on the squishy purple love seat. This was where I'd have to really work my magic.

I set the magazine and my hot chocolate down, turning my attention to him with a sly smile. He obviously didn't know what I was smiling at, which wasn't unexpected since I was simply doing it to throw him off base, but he returned it with his own grin, obviously understanding that something was about to happen in his favor. I laid my arm over the back of the chair so I could play with his hair while I talked to him.

"I'm really glad you came," I said softly, keeping my gaze trained on his. I had to buy some time and look pretty close to him since his girlfriend should be walking in any minute. I had given her specific instructions to watch for him from the bookstore across the street and come in about five minutes after him. Taylor seemed to like my slim fingers running through his hair, which he demonstrated by placing a tentative hand on my leg. I was almost worried that he'd suddenly become enthralled with my shoes and forget what we were doing here, but much to my relief he continued to look at me. Well, not really at me. More at my lips, but I took that as a good sign too, so I didn't try to bring his gaze back up to my eyes.

"I'm starting to think I'm pretty glad I came too," he replied. His reply was about thirty seconds too late for normal conversation, but I pretended not to notice and simply went on smiling, trying not to look to the door for my escape route. Even if I had wanted to look at the door, my line of sight would have been blocked by the pillar of angry girlfriend that now appeared next to me.

It took Taylor a minute to realize that Heather was standing right next to him, but I didn't hold that against him—the boy was effectively distracted, after all. Heather actually had to clear her throat to get his attention. Once she did this, however, the entire mood of the scene changed. Taylor went from looking like he was living in a state of ignorant bliss to looking like someone had just told him people were going to stop wearing shoes altogether—let alone stylish ones.

"Who's she?" I asked in my best oblivious voice. Heather simply glared down at me, and I had to hand it to her, I was actually pretty scared.

"She's just . . . um . . . wait, I thought you said she was your friend too?" he asked in a justifiably confused tone. All I could think in my head was, "Crap. There goes my career." How had I managed to overlook that glaring detail? Normally I'd act guilty and acknowledge that my friend had every right to be mad that I was out with her boyfriend, but this time I had just let words spill out of my mouth. I was really loosing my skill. I scrambled mentally to come up with some sort of explanation for my obvious mistake. Luckily I didn't have to try to answer for my slip-up because Heather began yelling quite loudly at Taylor. Although I had asked my clients not to cause a scene, I was grateful for this one. Taylor was so shocked by her sudden outburst I didn't think he'd ever have the chance to ask me to clarify my mistake.

Between Heather's bouts of shouting, I somehow managed to slip in an apology and slip out the door, leaving them to scream at each other in peace. Some of my clients just loved the drama aspect of my job. I offered them a way to get out of their relationship drama free, but there were always those ones who wanted a good scream-fest to finish things off with a bang.

I walked quickly to my car, hoping that if I could get home fast enough, I wouldn't even have to think about how badly I had been performing my job lately. I had never slipped up in the past, and now I seemed to be doing it with every client. I shook these thoughts from my mind and hurried home where I could change and concentrate on painting for a while.

Taking a few deep breaths and composing myself, I pulled my folding easel out from under my bed. I laid newspapers out all over my carpet and got everything ready to start painting.

My room was full of the other pieces I had painted, all of them different but with some unseen touch that made it evident they were mine. My favorite piece hung right above my bed. It had been a fun process to create this one, with its thick layers of paint that just made you want to touch it. The colors were mostly blues and greens, and I had used my fingers instead of brushes to give the surface that thick, worked up feel. It wasn't really a painting of anything in particular, just lots of swirling colors and squiggling lines.

Today, however, I was in a red mood. I mixed reds and oranges and yellows into hot fiery colors, which I layered thickly onto the small canvas. I made a circular sun with a spiral in the center and a long expanse of yellow sand that eventually made contact with the distant red shadowy mountains. It wasn't a masterpiece when I finished it about four hours later, but it was enough to exhaust me to the point that I fell asleep the moment my paint-covered face hit my clean pillow.

seven

I opened my eyes the next morning and saw the sun streaming through my window, which was the first sign that something was wrong. That horrible sinking feeling instantly hit my stomach, and I looked at my clock with dread. It told me, with unnerving calm, that it was 9:00, which meant that I was already an hour late for school. I jumped out of bed too quickly, filling my vision with a white cloud that only hindered my already cramped "getting ready" time. I cursed myself under my breath because I hadn't laid my clothes out the night before like I usually did.

Flinging open my closet, I looked over in my "punk" section for what I could wear that day. I yanked on some black cargo pants and a tight white tank top, deciding that with this boy, who was starting to look like a wild card, simple would be best. I pulled my short hair back into a little nub of a ponytail and quickly put some eyeliner on, scrubbing furiously at the paint on my cheek. The oversized black leather purse from yesterday wouldn't really work with my outfit today, so I quickly shoved everything into a basic black backpack and sprinted out the door with half of an untoasted bagel in my mouth.

The drive to school had never seemed so long, but I used the extra time to think about what I had to do today. I had lost my usual morning time where I would at least get to know the person I was breaking up with, which meant that if he threw me for a loop at all during break I could be in deep trouble. As I pulled into the parking lot, I realized that I had forgotten to bring my camera. So much for an ice breaker— I would just have to rely on my physical charms for this one and hope they would be sufficient to distract him long enough to deliver the news without too much pain. Judging by the red paint spot that had stayed defiantly on my cheek, though, my feminine wiles were a long shot.

Swallowing the rest of my bagel in one bite, I ran to the attendance office and explained why I was late to the skeptical woman there. She raised an eyebrow at my breathlessness and checked my file on her computer. Apparently she liked what she saw there because she said it was fine and just gave me a late slip to give my teacher. I didn't even get a reprimand. Maybe today wouldn't be as bad as I had originally thought.

I walked into my psychology class in the middle of a lab, so I didn't draw much attention to myself. Most of the other students had their faces pressed against microscopes, for which I was grateful. I didn't really understand why we'd need microscopes in psychology, unless Miss Tess was trying to cement the fact that it was, in fact, a science. I handed the late slip to my teacher who took it without question, and then I slunk back to my desk where an unoccupied microscope waited for me. The lab was confusing and required that I have some drawing skill, which, as I previously mentioned, I don't. I wasn't able to finish it by the time the bell rang for break, but most of the others weren't able to either.

I checked my face one last time in my compact, noting with pleasure that the paint was now completely gone from my cheek. David was in the same spot as yesterday, but today Claire was not clinging to him, which I knew was my cue to work my magic. I quickly put some lip-gloss on before I made my way over to my unsuspecting victim. He was behaving much like he had the day before, glancing around him as if he expected a bomb to suddenly fall from the sky. I tried to ignore this behavior and put on my alluring smile.

"Hey, you're David, right?" I asked the preoccupied boy innocently. He started a bit from my obviously unexpected greeting and quickly looked me over. I'm guessing he liked what he saw because a grin instantly spread across his face, and he seemed to relax.

"Yeah, I'm David. Who are you?" he asked simply. It was an easy enough question to answer but the fact that he wasn't blown away by my looks or dumbfounded by the fact that I'd just walked right up and talked to him was slightly disconcerting. I had, however, vowed not to lose my head like I had the day before, and so I forced myself to construct semi-coherent sentences.

"I'm Amelia," I said automatically, only to instantly realize I'd used my full name—my real, full name—and that was something I never did with my projects. It only complicated things if they had any valuable information on me. I smiled broadly to cover up my self-loathing and tried to move on from that small mistake, hoping that by some miracle he hadn't heard my name.

"Well, Amelia, what can I do for you?" This boy seemed to be brimming with confidence, which was always dangerous. I normally worked with boys who were easy to woo and, therefore, easy to break up with for their girlfriends. This boy, however, didn't seem to want to make my life easy. He had also said my name, turning my panic level up a notch. I tried to remember my usual story. Why had I always found an excuse to talk to these boys? Oh right. Fear-of-being-alone-syndrome.

"Well, I'm friends with your girlfriend, Claire, and she's sick today so I wanted to know if I could sit with you." I repeated the words as if I was reading them from a book, but I added my innocent smile, keeping my fingers crossed that I was convincing.

"You're friends with Claire?" he asked, sounding completely unconvinced.

"Yes?" Why had I just answered his question like a question? This was going horribly wrong. He smirked at this, keeping his eyes trained on me.

"Why haven't I ever seen you hanging around with her during school? I mean, if you have no one to sit with when she's sick, then wouldn't that mean you normally sat with her during break and lunch?" This boy was smart and persistent, I'd give him that. But I wasn't about to let him get the best of me. His questions were just making me angry now, and I refused to give a refund for the first time in my entire career.

"I actually just moved here from Pennsylvania," I said confidently, remembering that Claire had mentioned being born there. Granted, I knew nothing about the state, but I was counting on this being enough information for him. "We grew up together and my parents just decided to move out to California for work so Claire convinced them to let me come to Thousand Oaks High rather than being home-schooled." Had I given too much information? That was the downfall of lying; you always try to overcompensate for lack of truth with way too much fiction.

"Where in Pennsylvania are you from?" he asked

nonchalantly. What was he, a detective? "My family travels back that way a lot so maybe I've been to your hometown." It was now official. I hated this boy. He was snoopy and relentless, and my whole career was about to be exposed.

"Lancaster," I said automatically, naming the only city in Pennsylvania that I knew of. Incidentally, I had family living in Lancaster, California, only an hour from where I was standing at that very moment. Maybe after this boy ruined my career I'd go live with them and break hearts in the high desert.

"Lancaster?" he repeated slowly. "Isn't that where the Amish live?" Dang. I knew there was a reason I'd heard of that city before. I nodded my head deliberately and let my eyes stay locked on his, refusing to back down.

"Other people live there too," I said with finality. I'd already wasted five of my ten minutes trying to convince this boy I was actually Claire's friend. I might have to keep her sick for another day to get rid of this one. A new determination to rid myself of this pest firmly in place, I cleared my throat and got back to business. "So is it all right if I sit down, now that we've gone over my personal history?" The boy laughed softly and nodded his head. Finally, something was going my way. I sat next to him and was hit with an overwhelmingly wonderful scent. It had to be his cologne or shampoo or something, but whatever it was, it was unearthly.

"You smell really good," I said instantly, to which he raised an eyebrow. It was a perfectly normal response to a perfectly abnormal statement. I really had no idea what had made me say it and, looking back on it, that would have been a wonderful time to bow out gracefully and just forfeit this entire job. "Never mind," I mumbled, knowing there was no way to talk myself out of that one. No matter what stupid thing came out of my mouth next, at least I knew there were only five minutes left in the break.

"So, Amelia, where do you live?" This David seemed to say my name every time he spoke, as if just waiting for me to snap at him for having memorized it so quickly. And why on earth did he need to know where I lived?

"Excuse me?" I asked in what I hoped was a casual manner.

"You said you just moved here. Where did you move? Are you close to Claire?" Now that he had explained himself I guessed that it was a pretty reasonable question. It only presented one problem—I had no idea where Claire lived, so I couldn't make up an address near her. I only had one choice.

"I live about ten minutes south of the school, near the city library." My lack of a filter was simply stunning. Not only had I told this boy my real name, but I had given him a general idea of where I actually lived. This was not good for business at all, and something had to be done.

"Well, I need to get going," I finally said through gritted teeth. "Can't miss English . . . I'll see you at lunch." And with that I got up and quickly made my way to Mrs. Sanders' class. At least there I'd have two hours to pull myself together so I could finish the job without any more blunders.

Today, much to my relief, we were watching a movie about a book we'd just read. Thank goodness for burned-out high school teachers who would rather check their email while we watched a movie instead of actually teaching us something. Mrs. Sanders definitely looked exhausted, and there was a little rumor flitting around the school that she had recently taken to drinking large quantities of alcohol in her living room while trying to grade papers. This rumor probably wasn't true, since I didn't know a single person who would want to spend their Friday night hiding out in a teacher's living room, but it definitely made for interesting gossip. At least, it was good gossip for people who actually had friends to gossip with. I waved away my pang of self-pity and took a deep breath, preparing myself to dive headfirst into my newly developed problem named David while the rest of the class pretended to watch the reenactment of a classic novel.

All right, so, David knew my name and sort of knew where I lived. No big deal, I could always get rid of him quickly and just never answer my door again. This boy wouldn't pose a threat to my business or me because I wouldn't let him. Besides, he probably just liked me and wanted to get to know me more. I'd broken up with enough guys for enough girls to know how their minds worked. All I had to do was tell him his girlfriend wanted to break up with him. It wasn't that hard, just a few simple words, to be exact. And who cares if I don't do it gently and he gets his heart broken? Well . . . I suppose I did, and Claire did. The only reason I even have a job is so that boys don't get hurt by the breakup or at least don't feel like it was their girlfriend's fault. So just ending it without somehow making it seem all right was out of the question.

I tapped my thumb impatiently against the desk, causing a few people to turn and throw me dirty looks. I gave them a too-bright smile and continued tapping away, un-phased by their unvoiced threats. Besides, none of these people knew who I was anyway, and by next week I'd probably have a different hair color and personality. They probably just wondered why they kept getting a new student every week who sat in the same place in their English class.

When the bell finally rang for lunch, I had no real plan and absolutely no idea what I was doing. I bought a bag of chips and a bottle of water so that, if need be, I could stuff my face when David asked difficult questions, which I assumed he inevitably would. Seeing David, I sat down next to him, allowing myself to actually look at him and size up his threat level. David was definitely good looking; there was no denying that fact. Even someone like me who never noticed that kind of thing could tell that he would be the type of boy girls fell in love with and swore their favorite songs described perfectly. Today his shaggy blond hair hung in his eyes. He would absently run his fingers through it to get it out of the way, doing it all with a small crooked smile. He was wearing jeans and a long-sleeved black shirt, despite the day's perfect weather.

I decided that, while sitting next to him, I should probably just refrain from breathing because I could smell his perfect scent with every inhale. It wasn't even a smell that I could describe. It was just perfect. It had the sharp dominance of cologne, with the soft undertones of a person's natural aroma. No matter what I called it, it was wonderful. And it was definitely clouding my head and making my job much more difficult. This boy had to go. Steeling myself, I turned to face him, ignoring his brilliant green eyes.

"So Claire and I have been hanging out a lot lately and I think she—"

"Do you want to go out with me sometime?" His interruption was so sudden and so final that I had to actually sit there for a minute and think about what he'd just said.

"Maybe this weekend?" he went on. "We could go grab a bite to eat." I furrowed my brow and tilted my head to the side in confusion, still not comprehending his words.

"What about Claire?" I asked, suddenly finding my voice again.

"Oh her? We broke up earlier today. It just wasn't

working out. So how about it? I mean, I'm sure it makes me seem like a pretty big jerk to ask you out right after I broke up with your friend but I think you're really interesting." His words were spoken in English and I was sure they were forming complete sentences, but I still couldn't understand anything he was saying.

"You broke up with Claire?" was all I could manage.

"Yeah. I don't know if she's said anything to you but we haven't been getting along very well lately." I shook my head dumbly, not really sure what I was shaking it at.

"Yeah but *you* broke up with *her*?" He nodded more slowly this time, as if I wouldn't understand what the gesture meant if he sped it up—which was probably true. But what I couldn't understand was what this meant for me. Did I fail in my job? Would Claire be mad? Was this amazingly good-looking boy really asking me out? Would that be ethical to go somewhere with a job? All of these questions raced through my mind, muddling it so completely that I didn't even notice when the bell rang for biology.

"I'll just take that as a yes and see you at eight on Saturday." And with that he was gone, and I was screwed.

eight

The next day David was nowhere to be found at school. I didn't spot him at his usual hangout and when I asked his friends they said he hadn't come to school that day. Was it possible he was avoiding me so that I couldn't call the date off, or was I just being paranoid? Either way, it was a very bad thing that I couldn't get a hold of him. But then again, he couldn't contact me either, could he? He didn't have my phone number or address, so I should be fine. Letting this knowledge relax me a little, I went to my locker to find my history book, even though we probably wouldn't need it for our promisingly boring lecture. At my locker stood a tall, skinny blonde girl in a cheerleading outfit. Her short hair was curled into tight ringlets and framed her face nicely. She leaned against my locker and tapped her foot impatiently as I approached. I obviously wasn't walking fast enough for her.

She looked me up and down quickly, taking in my appearance and apparently gauging whether or not I could handle whatever she was about to throw at me. I smiled uneasily at her and stopped just short of my locker, hoping she'd either say what she had to say or get out of my way so I could get my stuff for class.

"Are you Amelia?" she asked, her voice appropriately haughty for someone of her high school social rank.

"Yeah, did you want to hire me for something?" To any normal passerby this probably would have sounded like an odd response to her question, but I had grown good at reading people and knowing when they were coming to me for a job— that, and there was the small fact that I had no friends and no one knew who I was. The cheerleader's face lit up considerably at my words; she apparently hadn't been convinced that I actually existed and was relieved to find that there really was someone who would save her from social awkwardness.

"Yeah, I need you to break up with my boyfriend Blane for me." She handed over some information on the boy, and I dug my normal required fact sheet from my locker and gave it to her in turn.

"I need you to fill that out and give it to me tomorrow, along with a picture of the boy and your phone number so I can call you for any further information I need," I said mechanically. The cheerleader gave me an odd look at this statement but didn't say anything and simply took the paper.

"Um, Blane likes blondes . . . is that a problem?"

I laughed at this statement and shook my head.

"I'll change it tonight. You do know I'm charging fifty, since it's so close to prom, right?" She simply nodded and handed over a wad of cash. I counted it quickly and stuck out my hand. She shook it with a smile and the deal was made.

I didn't spot David at all that day, which worried me beyond all belief. If I couldn't find him by tomorrow, then there was actually a chance that this boy would somehow show up on my doorstep on Saturday. Even without knowing my address, I wouldn't put it past him to mysteriously know exactly where I lived without having to ask anyone. This fact was unsettling and the burning blonde color stripper in my hair didn't help to ease my discomfort. I always hated having to go from black to blonde overnight. It sometimes left my hair with an orange-ish tint that took a while to cover up. Tonight though, the fates smiled on me, and my hair turned a prissy platinum blonde without leaving me bald.

I removed the black nail polish and replaced it with bright pink, which meant I had to walk around my room with those uncomfortable foam toe separators on my feet while spreading my fingers like some sort of flying squirrel trying to take off. I skimmed through my extensive wardrobe and picked out a white pleated skirt that cut off several inches above my knee and a bubblegum pink tank top. I threw some hot pink stiletto heels into the mix and was done with my work assignment for that night.

Lexi Monroe, which turned out to be the cheerleader's name (though I would have been just fine calling her cheerleader), had managed to send a picture of her soon-to-be-ex-boyfriend from her phone to my email address. I hadn't given her my email address, but since it was simply my full name, I guess it wasn't that hard to figure it out. Her resourcefulness did surprise me, though. So, with her picture and fact sheet to guide me, I figured I could start this project tomorrow, even though I usually avoided working on a Friday, since it could sometimes run over into my uneventful weekends. This was my exception. I had to get back on my game or I was doomed. All right, so maybe I wasn't doomed, but I was definitely in danger of losing my self-confidence.

I glanced at the fact sheet before me and tried to think of my plan of attack.

Name—Blane
Age—18
POI—Football, Parties, Cars
Deadline—Tuesday

Though the deadline was slightly shocking, his POIs were almost laughably predictable. It was like a jock stereotype straight out of a movie. I looked them over one more time to make sure I hadn't invented them simply by expecting them to be there, and sure enough, there they were in all of their unsubstantial glory. Then again, I suppose someone without an original thought in her head doesn't have much room to make fun of the interests of others.

I shook my head, figuring I could lure this one away simply by bending over in front of him in my less-than-modest skirt. It was definitely the easy way out, but Lexi never specified how I had to get rid of him, just that it had to be done so that his best friend could ask her to prom.

I checked the number on the fact sheet so that I could confirm tomorrow's breakup with Lexi. There's nothing worse then trying to break up with a boy and having their girlfriend show up halfway through. I dialed the number on my now pink cell phone.

"This is Lex," said a chipper voice. I wondered why on earth she'd need to shorten Lexi. After all, wasn't Lexi the shortened version of Alexis or something? Perhaps the four letters were still too strenuous for her, and she needed the three letters to keep it simple.

"Hey Lexi, it's Amelia," I said professionally. "I was just calling to confirm that you won't be in school tomorrow so that I can get rid of Blane for you."

"What? No you can't do it tomorrow! He's throwing a party this weekend and I want to be able to say good-bye properly."

This news shocked me slightly, and I didn't even want to think about what her last statement entailed, so I simply said, "Really? Well, if you need it done by Tuesday I should start working on it."

"I don't care. I thought you did this stuff in one day anyway? Why can't you just do it Monday?" I sighed deeply and tried to control my temper. Some people really thought I was a miracle worker—they never took into account illness, or the fact that not all breakups take one neat little forty-minute lunch break.

"If you want me to start on Monday then I'm going to have to ask you to move the deadline to Wednesday as a precaution." There was some audible grumbling on the other line, which annoyed me, but she finally gave in.

"Fine. Do whatever you need to do." Then the line went dead. She had hung up on me. My annoyance wasn't at the fact that she was being ungrateful and unrealistic, but rather the fact that she didn't seem to think that I could possibly lure her boyfriend away from a catch as great as her. I rolled my eyes at the cheerleader's unjustified confidence and tossed my phone into the big white leather purse I'd been planning to use for school tomorrow.

It then instantly struck me that I didn't have a job tomorrow. David had broken up with Claire, so I didn't have to worry about him, and I couldn't start work on Blane until Monday. I could wear whatever I wanted tomorrow. But what on earth did I want to wear? I rarely dressed for myself. The only time I wasn't working was usually weekends and then I'd just stay in sweats and paint for two days straight. With this exciting new prospect of dressing myself in mind, I opened up my closet and looked through the many different styles.

I finally settled for nondescript blue jeans, a gray fitted T-shirt, some black and white tennis shoes, and a long, thin, white muslin scarf. I completed this outfit with a knitted white beret to stuff my newly dyed blonde hair into. Tomorrow I was definitely going for invisible, and maybe that way David wouldn't find me and he'd forget about our "date."

The next day at school I was met with a very unwelcome sight at my locker, which looked like it was turning into a meeting spot for my clients. Claire stood, arms crossed over her chest, eyes burning a hole through my head. I approached cautiously, not quite sure what I'd done to merit this less-than-congenial greeting.

"What do you think you're doing?" she asked in a furious whisper. I threw her an honestly puzzled look while I tried to make sure no one was listening to us.

"What are you talking about?"

"David!" she said simply. Her statement was so sudden that I thought perhaps he was standing behind me. I looked over my shoulder to see the normal procession of students passing through the hallway.

"Not behind you, you idiot. What did you do? I paid you fifty dollars to break up with him for me!"

"You guys are broken up," I said shakily, finding that this confrontation was taking a lot of the fight out of me. I suspected that it had something to do with the fact that I didn't have an identity that day. I wasn't Lia the super cheerleader, or Mari the independent punk chick. I was Amelia Marie Bedford, sixteen-year-old breakup artist and personality-less high school student.

"Yeah, I wanted *you* to break up with him for me. Not the other way around! What am I supposed to do now? It looks like he dumped me!" she screeched. We were now attracting some attention, which was something I strictly avoided doing when I was off the clock.

"Why does that matter? You got what you wanted. You and David are broken up and you can get what's-his-name to ask you to the prom."

"It's my reputation, Amelia," she spat. "I know you don't have one, but I can't go around having people break up with me. It doesn't sit well with my image. You need to fix this."

"Fix this?" I repeated incredulously. "How am I supposed to do that?"

"Make it look like I broke up with him," she answered simply, as if it were the most obvious thing in the world.

"Why don't you do that yourself? Just tell your friends that's what happened." I had no idea where any of this was going, but I knew I didn't like it.

"I paid you to save my reputation!"

"No, you paid me to avoid an awkward situation for yourself," I quickly corrected her. I may have suddenly turned spineless, but I wasn't about to give back the fifty dollars she'd given me just because she had a bruised ego.

"Whatever. You need to get David to go out with me again so I can break up with him properly and publicly, or I'm taking my money back." Her threat was loud and clear, and all I could do was nod silently. She turned to walk away but called over her shoulder, "And you should fix whatever you did to your hair. You look like Lexi Monroe."

That school day went by in a haze of commotion. My mind was completely wrapped around my current problem and I didn't pay attention to a single word out of my teachers' mouths. My stomach was all tied up in knots over the prospect of A) getting David to ask Claire back out, B) getting her to break up with him publicly so I wouldn't have to give the money back, and C) possibly sabotaging any chance I had with David. Though, all things considered, I'd say that would be the best part of this whole plan. I couldn't risk having a crush on a boy. Besides, what boy would ever be okay with his girlfriend flirting with a new guy every day?

I wasn't at all surprised to find that my mother was

having another "client dinner" this Friday, so I ate some cold macaroni and cheese straight out of the fridge without even heating it up. I finished up my homework for the weekend and tried to watch reruns of old black-and-white TV shows until I fell asleep. As it turned out, however, even Lucy's antics couldn't soothe me, so I ended up going online to try to cyber stalk David. I needed some information on this boy, and I already had his name, which meant I should be able to find some sort of online profile for him. Everyone seems to have their own website now, which makes things infinitely easier for me when a client doesn't give me enough information about their dear boyfriends.

I went to a search engine and typed in "David Fields" in an attempt to locate my burden's website. I found many photography websites and even an interesting blog or two, but nothing from this boy at school. Now things were really getting weird. As I've previously stated, everyone has a website. Everyone. To find someone without some sort of online profile is like finding someone who doesn't exist . . . at least in high school.

I considered calling Claire up just to confirm that I had the right last name, but I had a violent flashback to our last conversation and decided against it. Now all that was left to do was go to bed, hope I could get through the weekend without this boy single-handedly ruining my career, and paint a picture or two. Should be easy enough.

nine

Saturday morning I let myself sleep in until eleven. I had tossed and turned all night, so waking up at eleven felt more like waking up at three in the morning. I stumbled out of bed, rubbing my eyes and yawning. Then I tripped over the big square fan that I had aimed at my bed the night before. I glared at the inanimate object and went into the bathroom to get ready for my Saturday in the way I always did. I pulled my short hair back into a now-blonde ponytail, washed my face, and brushed my teeth. I didn't bother changing out of my sweats, even though I had a slight nagging feeling that David might actually appear at my house. I refused to let myself believe that this typical high school boy would be resourceful enough to find me. And so, stubborn resolve firmly set, I went downstairs to have an early lunch.

"Someone slept in late," my mother said as I thumped down the stairs.

"Someone stayed out late," I countered, throwing her a suspicious glance.

"Client dinner," she said simply. I rolled my eyes at her retreating form, wondering when she'd think I was old enough to know she actually had a dating life. Maybe she thought that I would be jealous, since I didn't have one of my own. Or maybe she assumed I harbored some affectionate feelings for the man who left us for no reason in particular. Either way, I couldn't find any good explanation as to why she'd hide things from me, but that wasn't my biggest problem right now. Right now my biggest problem was David, with my growling stomach coming in at a close second.

"I brought some fettuccine Alfredo back from the restaurant last night. You're welcome to eat it. I have to work this weekend, but I'll see you tonight," my mother called from the front door.

"I might not be home tonight," I said suddenly. I hadn't meant to say it, just like I didn't mean to say every word that came out of my mouth when I was sitting with David. Things seemed to pour from my mouth lately in some relentless deluge.

"Oh?" my mom responded, as a way of being inquisitive.

"Date," I went on, still unsure of why I was spewing lies at my mother, who had been kind enough to bring me fettuccini Alfredo.

"Oh," she said again, this time in a slightly deflated manner, which didn't make any sense. "Job related?" she pried.

"No," I answered. We both seemed to be suddenly incapable of constructing any sentence longer than two words. There was a long pause, and I knew by instinct that my mom was probably looking down at her watch to gauge how much time she had to pull some more information out of me.

"Have fun at work," I finally called, cutting off the conversation before she could ask any more questions about my fictitious date—or at least what I hoped was a fictitious date. The door clicked closed, and I heard my mother's car pulling away from the house. I breathed a sigh of relief for having escaped the exchange relatively unharmed and then proceeded to reheat the pasta my mom had brought me.

Sitting on the floor in the middle of my room, I picked through tubes of paint, throwing away the dry ones and salvaging what could be salvaged. I ate my pasta with chopsticks just to liven the meal up a bit, an action that had always amused my mother. Anything that hinted at a personality all my own made her happy. I think she sometimes thought her daughter was a sociopath or a future con artist or something along those lines.

I kicked a blue paint tube with my foot so that it rolled into the "useable" pile on the floor and threw my paper plate away once the pasta was all gone. Stretching in the way that a lazy person does on a lazy day, I fell onto my back and lay on the floor, staring up at the ceiling and thinking about the mess I'd gotten myself into. I wondered how far Claire would go to make herself feel better. Would she just take the money back or would she expose exactly what I do, making it impossible for me to continue on in my body of work. Neither option sounded like much fun for me, which meant I had to figure out a way to solve this David problem.

From a remote corner of my purse on my bed, I could hear a buzzing sound. It was my phone. Reaching in and grabbing the pink plastic device, I was informed that I had one unread text message. My mom didn't really know how to text, and when she did it took her a long time, which meant that it probably wasn't her. I highly doubted that the paint supply shop would text me, since I only had their landline. And I hoped more than I'd ever hoped for anything before that it wasn't Claire, sending me an angry reminder of just how much trouble I was in.

I flipped open the phone to find that the message was from a number I didn't recognize. I opened the text tentatively and read my mysterious message from its mysterious sender.

"Don't forget. 8 p.m. tonight."

"David?" I asked my phone, as if it would reply to my question. It didn't. I quickly saved the number for future reference and groaned in dismay. I had actually convinced myself that he would forget all about our "date" and I could just deal with him at school. I suppose, though, that I should have been more concerned with the fact that he had somehow obtained my number and that he would somehow be showing up on my doorstep at eight o'clock tonight.

I went over numerous excuses in my head as to why I wouldn't be able to go on the date, until it struck me that this might actually be my chance to set things right. If I spent the whole date convincing him that he should be Claire's boyfriend, then perhaps by the time Monday rolled around my only concern would be getting rid of the jock for Lexi.

"Okay, so this is good," I said to my empty room, nodding at nothing in particular. Yep, the stress this whole ordeal had brought on was definitely causing me to lose my mind. I quickly got up off the ground and went to my closet, ready to find a perfect "date" outfit. The only dates I had ever gone on were with boys who I had just broken up with for their girlfriends. I was always in character then and didn't have to worry about how I looked—as long as I fit the mold of what they had always been attracted to, I was just fine.

Tonight, however, was a completely different matter. I had to look unattractive enough that he wouldn't try to continue hitting on me, while looking attractive enough that he'd actually listen to what I was saying. It was a shame how much appearance really factored in to what your opinion meant to someone, but that was the reality and that was what I had to play with. I figured that for tonight I should go with something relatively inoffensive, something generic and nondescript, but still stylish and eye-catching.

I thumbed through my clothes quickly, noting with dismay that it was already two o'clock in the afternoon. It wasn't that I really thought I'd need six hours to get ready for a date where I would be convincing the guy that he didn't want to date me; I simply wanted some extra time to do some mental preparation. I had to construct a plan, and I had to solidify exactly what I was going to do.

I decided on a jean skirt that came to just above my knee, with black cut-off tights underneath it. I did, after all, have to remember who my audience was and what kind of girls he apparently liked to date. Or in this case, what type he liked to break up with. I completed the outfit with a black baby doll T-shirt and black flip-flops. There was nothing special about my outfit, but it had just enough "date" quality to it.

Setting these clothes out on my bed I headed for the bathroom to take a shower, which was a rare occurrence for a Saturday. I usually avoided any form of getting ready on Saturdays—the process just took away from the magic of being lazy. After a very long, very hot shower, I got ready in a deliberate manner. I took extra time curling my shoulder-length blonde hair and even did my makeup with careful precision, lining my eyes so that the amount of liner used actually matched from the right side to the left. The silvery black shadow I used on my lids made the blue in my eyes really stand out. Deep down I felt a sort of excited anticipation about the date, even though it wasn't really my date. It was Claire's date. Despite this little fact glaring at me, I still allowed myself to feel some excitement over getting ready to spend the evening with a particularly gorgeous boy.

ten

It was a little after four o'clock by the time I finished with my shower, hair, and makeup and I was ready to get into costume. As I pulled the short jean skirt on, I didn't feel the same way I always felt when dressing like someone else. I almost felt a sense of self that I hadn't experienced since I was little like I was actually doing something just for me and not just for a client. I quickly shook these thoughts from my head, however, knowing they led to dangerous territory that my future college education couldn't afford to explore.

Looking myself over in the mirror I had to admit I actually looked pretty good. With my blonde curly hair and the neat, dark makeup, I looked like a mix between a '50s actress and a rock star. The effect was nice, and I gave myself a mental pat on the back. As much as I wanted to whip out my paint set and get to work on a very round, very pink, colorful expressionist piece, I refrained, deciding that I didn't want to show up for the date looking like something Jackson Pollock had gotten a hold of.

With three hours to go until the blessed event began, I went over some ideas in my head. I figured I could talk to him for a bit, strictly for professional purposes of course, before getting to Claire. I could ask why they broke up, put some doubts into his head about his decision, suggest that maybe she missed him a little, and even plant the idea of getting them back together right in his subconscious. It shouldn't really be that difficult, in all reality. It was the job I normally did, just in reverse.

With that obstacle out of the way, I tackled another difficult decision. Should I eat before I went on the date? Eight o'clock was a bit late for dinner, but what if he waited to eat so he could take me out somewhere? Or even worse, what if he didn't, and my growling stomach gave away my pathetic assumption that we would be getting dinner? What on earth would we do if we didn't get dinner? Why were we starting this date so late? Did dates normally start at eight o'clock?

My head was swimming with questions, and I didn't have the desire to answer any of them. All I wanted to do was get this date over with and accomplish my goal so I wouldn't have to be confused about my feelings or my future in this career anymore. It seemed as though things had been going downhill ever since I'd taken on this new job. It was almost like someone was trying to sabotage what I did for a living. Of course, that was probably just the paranoia talking. The paranoia and the hunger.

I don't really remember what I did for those three long hours while I waited for David to appear on my doorstep, but I'm pretty sure it involved alphabetizing all of the CDs clients had given to me and then categorizing them by genre. I had a vague determination to make my life easier and thought that this would be the perfect way to get into character quickly for my various jobs.

At eight o'clock sharp, the doorbell rang. I let out a little gasp, the kind you emit when you watch a scary movie and you just know something is going to pop out of that dark alley and yet it gets you every time. I had actually been watching the clock, and it was a welcome shock when the doorbell sounded just as eight o'clock flickered to life on the digital screen. I stood up quickly and looked myself over in the mirror to make sure my makeup hadn't migrated down my face into a pool of black under my eyes. Everything seemed to be in order, and I looked just as good as I had three hours earlier when the epic CD organizing had begun.

I snatched my black leather purse from my bed and headed down the hallway to the front door. We didn't have one of those front doors with glass in them so that the people outside can awkwardly see you approaching from a distance, and right now, I was happy for that. For all David knew, I was taking my sweet time because I wasn't really that interested. I tiptoed to the peephole so that it wouldn't sound like I had walked up to the door, only to stop for some odd amount of time. Looking through the little opening, I saw him standing there in all his glory. The porch light shone down on him, making him look like an angel, which I'm sure is a pretty cheesy comparison, but at that moment it worked quite nicely. He ran his fingers through his hair like he had when I'd been sitting next to him. There was just something about guys doing that—it gave them some sort of unspoken confidence in my eyes, like they were on top of the world and had everything. It seemed like the only thing they could think of to complete their perfection was running their fingers through their hair. (Because that logic makes complete sense.)

Finally, after what may have actually been an hour of peering at David through this little hole and seriously considering turning right around and going back to my room, I opened the door. He looked mildly surprised, but proud of himself. I assumed the pride was for finding my address and my phone number when I didn't have any friends. He looked me up and down for a moment with a look on his face that I really couldn't decipher, and believe me; I've seen many different looks on boy's faces when they look at me. I waited for the inevitable "You look nice" or "I like that skirt on you" or even the more frequent but less acceptable "You look hot," but instead he simply said, "Ready?"

I nodded dumbly at his question, a little hurt that he didn't comment at all on my appearance, and a little happy that he might have actually been interested in something other than that. I did, however, have to quickly remind myself that he couldn't have possibly been interested in my personality since I tragically didn't have one. Or at least, I didn't have one of my own. I had whatever personality my clients wanted me to have.

I followed David outside to his car, which was an old little blue thing. I had no idea what kind of car it was, just that it was slightly rusty, which I found a bit shocking. David seemed very well put together and clean, and I couldn't imagine him driving something that wasn't as spotless as his sweaters. He opened my door, which was always a good sign, and then took his spot in the driver's seat. After he had started the car and begun driving in the general direction of the school, I finally spoke, breaking the long silence between us.

"So where exactly are we going tonight?" He looked over at me as if just noticing I was there and smiled.

"I thought we'd grab some dinner. Unless, of course, you've already eaten. I mean, it is eight o'clock and everything." Well at least he wasn't a complete weirdo. He knew that dinner should definitely be eaten earlier than eight. My stomach growled right on cue, answering his question without me saying a word. "So what kind of food do you like?" he asked me, keeping his eyes trained ahead on the road. That question was completely pointless. He would have been much better off asking what kind of food I didn't like, because that list was much smaller.

"I like any food that's edible," I replied with a grin.

"So no seafood then?" he asked, the smallest of smiles creeping onto his strong features.

"I take it you're not a fan?" I asked. He pulled a face at my question, scrunching his nose up in disgust.

"All right, no seafood then. What about Italian? Pasta is good at any time of the day." In fact, I had a particular love of pasta for breakfast, but we didn't need to let David see my little oddities when this date wasn't even mine to jeopardize.

"Italian it is," he said with a small nod. I was half surprised when he kept going straight instead of turning on the road to go to our school. I was definitely on autopilot. This little shock only reminded me of how much I didn't get out of the house, increasing this date's potential by a few notches.

"Nice hair, by the way," David said after a few moments of silence.

"What?" I asked, completely puzzled by his statement. It didn't dawn on me until after my brilliant response that I had dyed my hair since I'd last seen him. For me it was typical to look in the mirror and see a different hair color every few days, and my mom had long since gotten used to it, but to normal people it must be quite a shock when my hair constantly changed at a breakneck pace.

"It's blonde," he pointed out, as if this little fact had possibly escaped my notice. Maybe he thought I had been ambushed in the middle of the night by the hair-dye fairy and the result had simply floated right by my scope of understanding.

"Yeah . . . I get bored easily," I mumbled, hoping this explanation would save me from any further questions.

"I like it," he said finally. All right, so he was a blonde guy. Maybe if I could get Claire to change her hair color it would be easier for me to get them back together. This thought only made me realize how weird my job really is. Most of my date thus far had consisted of me covering up my job and thinking about how I could get my date back together with his ex-girlfriend, who I'd tried to get him to break up with originally. Good thing I had a psychology class, or I might need some serious therapy from all of this.

After a few more lies and some close calls on my part, we pulled into the parking lot of a small Italian restaurant. I could smell the breadsticks before we even entered the little building. The interior was dimly lit by fake candles with soft mood music maintaining the atmosphere. The host seated us in a cozy booth surprisingly close to the kitchen. I could hear the clattering of dishes and calling out of food orders from my seat. We looked at our menus, ordered drinks, and then were faced with the awkward silence first dates are famous for causing. This time in a date was normally just fine for me, because I would be strategically planning out how to get rid of the guy for good, while my date would be nervously contemplating my silence, wondering if it meant I didn't like him, or if I was feeling bad that he had just broken up with his girlfriend.

This date, however, was different. My half of the silence was spent in nervous anticipation. I knew there was nothing for me to be excited about, because the sole reason I was here was to manipulate this boy without his knowledge. But still, I couldn't help but feel that this date was a small reward for my years of work. Maybe this boy actually liked me and things could somehow work out. Of course, like all good dreams, these thoughts were instantly stifled by reality.

"So, Amelia, do you work?" I nearly choked on my soda

at his question, and I actually had to take a minute to recover from the coughing fit this unexpected turn in the conversation brought on. He looked at me with mild amusement, which was slightly disconcerting since I was, in fact, choking. Well, perhaps I wasn't choking, but I was sure coughing enough to cause other diners alarm. And here was my date, sitting there smirking at me like some cruel model from a clothing advertisement. After I regained my composure and patted my face with my maroon cloth napkin, I shook my head.

"No, I don't work," I said hoarsely, my voice still a bit scratchy from the violent coughing from a moment ago. I was amazed at how easy it was for me to lie. Not just to this boy, but to everyone. It seemed like a natural talent that I possessed, though I wasn't sure if that was really something I should be proud of. David raised an eyebrow. Then after a moment of what I figured was contemplation over this, his face softened and he reacted, however late, to my distress.

"Are you all right?" His face still held the smirk but his voice held a certain amount of compassion now. I looked at him incredulously. Not only had he practically been laughing as I choked on my soda, but he was now asking if I was all right after we'd moved on from my little drinking attack. This was something that I had to deal with in only my most socially inept clients; I hadn't expected this level of odd timing from David.

"Yeah, I'm fine," I answered, sounding almost suspicious. Maybe he was trying to make me think he was some social outcast so I wouldn't be so obviously pathetic about my interest in him. Then again, maybe he was just concerned and couldn't ask once I'd stopped choking because I'd blurted out my answer to his question as if it were a matter of life and death.

"Perhaps next time you should try drinking instead of inhaling," he commented dryly. I was about to shoot him an annoyed look when I caught the rueful gleam in his eye, signaling to me that it was a joke. I smiled back at him, and he broke into a soft laugh. Maybe this date wasn't going as disastrously as it seemed.

"So what about you?" I asked, taking a bite out of a warm breadstick and savoring the garlic taste. "Do you have some sort of job after school?"

"No official job really. I do write for the school newspaper, though. I don't get paid or anything, but I figure it's close enough to job training, so it counts. Occasionally I'll submit a piece for the local paper."

"Oh, wow, so do you want to be a journalist?" I suppose the answer to that should have been fairly obvious, but I was being slightly less than observant tonight. He laughed softly again, a sound I was quickly beginning to like.

"Yeah, I've always wanted to write for a newspaper. My brother makes fun of me because I got the idea of being a newspaper writer from Lois Lane."

"Wait, the girl from Superman?" I asked, amusement creeping into my voice.

"Yeah," he mumbled, looking down at his napkin. He had obviously been through this discussion before. "My brother always says I'll be the best Lois Lane at the paper." He rolled his eyes at the memory, and I tried to stifle a laugh.

"Well, when you get your first official job, I'll get you some heels that'll make the green in your eyes just pop," I said, putting on the best overly feminine voice I could muster. He shot me a playful death glare just as the waitress came to take our order.

I ordered spaghetti, a nice generic meal that wouldn't cause anyone to pass judgment. I was used to being generic.

I had conditioned myself so well to order only things that wouldn't draw any attention to my real personality (if it even existed) that it had become a habit. I had never had a problem with who I was, or wasn't, before this. I didn't have a personality and that was fine because I didn't need one to get by. I didn't need friends or hobbies, likes or dislikes—all I needed was something I was good at, and that thing was molding myself into whomever I needed to be. So why was it such a big deal now that I was the way I was?

I didn't hear what David ordered because I was too caught up in my own psychoanalysis. In fact, I hadn't even noticed that he was saying my name, possibly repeating it because I hadn't heard it the first time. His voice had that tone you use when you're trying to snap someone out of a daydream and it isn't working. I finally looked up at him with a puzzled expression glued to my face.

"Huh?" I said, sounding very intelligent, I'm sure.

"What's on your mind?" he asked, taking note of my dazed expression.

"Spaghetti," I said automatically, then mentally slapped myself on the wrist. The oddest things just seemed to pop out of my mouth around David. I really needed to concentrate and rein in all of my weirdness before he realized I really wasn't a "cool" person. Maybe this was it. Maybe David brought out my real personality and my real personality just happened to be a loser.

"All right, I'm just not going to ask then," he said, his mouth forming a thin-lipped smile as he shook his head, apparently amused. He looked down at his water glass for a moment, giving me enough time to compose myself and get back into what I was really supposed to be doing.

"So I talked to Claire today," I said cautiously, trying to nonchalantly play with the sugar packets on the table so that I didn't seem interested in the conversation.

"Oh, yeah?" he replied, and I could automatically tell he was using the same carefully-not-interested tone as me. "How is she?"

"She sounded a little down," I said with the slightest glance in his direction. He was staring at me intently, which caught me off guard. With his voice so distant and disinterested, I'd been expecting him to be doing some useless, distracting thing with his hands. Or I figured he would be looking at his placemat like it was the most interesting thing in the world. Instead, here he was, watching me. It made me nervous, instantly putting me on my guard so that I was doubly careful of my tone and expression. I returned my gaze to the sugar packed and pressed on. "I know this is personal but I thought you guys were really cute together. Why did you break up in the first place?"

On a normal date this would have been completely unacceptable territory to have stepped into, but I figured that by this point we both knew this wasn't a normal date—he with his odd reactions to my behavior and me . . . well, just me in general. He kept his gaze focused on me as a slight grin crept over his lips.

"I don't really want to talk about it," he answered. And with that the subject was closed. For now. I figured I could just bring it up again later on, maybe once we got back into the car so that he wouldn't have an escape from the situation. I nodded in understanding and pushed the sugar packet around the tabletop with my finger intently. "Since we're talking about relationships though," he began, instantly grabbing my attention. This couldn't be going anywhere good. "How has your dating life been? I mean other than right now, of course? You said you just moved here from Pennsylvania, right? So I'm assuming you really haven't dated much since getting here."

I was beginning to wonder if David somehow knew what I did for a living. It seemed like every question he aimed at me was meant specifically to tear down my nerves until I broke down and spilled the truth to him. Unless these really were normal first-date questions and I was just way out of the loop.

"No I haven't. I don't really like to date. In fact, I'd rather be alone most of the time." That's right; I was going to cut this thing off before it got any worse. I'd just show him how unavailable I was, then suggest Claire again and get the heck out of there. "I'm kind of a social recluse." I smiled brightly at him, daring him to ask any more questions that would hint at the real reason I was there. Surprisingly, he didn't make a snide remark or try to ask me anymore unanswerable questions. Instead he put up his hands in surrender and smiled.

After he had graciously backed off, an awkward silence fell over us. Though this kind of thing normally didn't bother me, I decided to give him a break since he had just done that for me. "So what kind of stuff do you submit to the local paper?"

He looked up at me as if he were surprised by my question but quickly composed himself and shrugged his shoulders. "A lot of different stuff, I guess," he said noncommittally. "I've done some human interest pieces, and some opinion pieces . . . a few others but that's about it."

"That's funny, because I would have pegged you for more of the 'bearer of bad news' type—obituaries, accidents, children getting little puppies stolen away from them—that sort of thing." I grinned at him, feeling pretty proud of myself for my clever joke until I saw the look his face had taken on. His lazy smile instantly melted into that look that women get when you ask them if they're pregnant when they're definitely not. I couldn't understand this reaction, and I was desperately hoping that he would crack a smile any minute and say "Gotcha!" but that didn't happen. He just continued to look at me as if I had run over his dog until I couldn't take his gaze anymore. I let my eyes drop to the pattern on the table, cleared my throat awkwardly, and muttered a quick "Sorry," under my breath, though I had no idea what I was sorry about.

The rest of our time in the restaurant went the way most dates do. We got our food and I tried desperately not to splash red sauce all over myself. He asked about my favorite color and my favorite movie, both of which I lied about, since I didn't really have a favorite anything. I asked him the same generic questions back, and when the bill came I offered to pay for myself even though I had no intention of actually doing that. I wasn't even sure if I had my wallet with me. But he chivalrously paid and we left.

In the car it looked like he was heading back to my house, cutting our date short. I guess that meant I had at least succeeded in making myself unappealing to him, so that threat was out of the way. Now I just had to work on getting him back together with Claire, and I had a whole fifteen-minute car ride for that.

"Hey, David?" I started sheepishly, actually a bit wary of the conversation we were about to have. I didn't want to have to do this, and I hadn't really come up with some brilliantly subtle way of saying it, so it was going to be rocky.

"Yeah?" he said, turning a radiant smile in my direction. I ignored the fact that I actually wanted that smile to be for me and pressed on with my tactless plea.

"Will you please just do me a favor and call Claire? Just talk to her? I know it would make her really happy." I was begging and I knew it. It wasn't just the fifty dollars that I didn't want to give up, it was my pride. If I couldn't finish this job properly, it would be my first official failure. I didn't think I could handle that label. I kept my eyes trained out the front windshield, afraid to see his reaction. There was a long moment of silence before I heard him sigh.

"Yeah, I'll call her," he promised quietly. I tried to keep my face smooth as the relief and happiness washed over me, mixing with the jealousy and anger that I was actually forcing this boy out of my life. The need to have him there was, I had to admit, completely shallow. I really didn't know much about him except that he liked to write and he was extremely good looking. I didn't even like blonds most of the time but his sandy hair looked beautiful when he constantly shook it away from his green eyes.

"Thanks," I replied sullenly. He caught the unhappiness in my tone and looked over at me inquiringly, but I just let out a small laugh and waved away his unspoken question with my hand. When he got to my house I hastily got out of the car and said a quick, "Thanks for dinner," over my shoulder. If I didn't get right out and go right up to my house, I would probably do something else stupid, like tell him that I changed my mind and that he shouldn't call Claire. Wasn't I leading him back into an inevitably painful relationship with Claire just to save my pride? It was the exact same thing Claire was about to do to him. I began walking quickly to my door when I felt a hand close around my elbow and a figure appeared beside me. David smiled winningly at me and began the trek to my doorstep.

"I can't very well let you walk yourself to the doorstep, now can I? That wouldn't make me a gentleman." I swallowed back the anxiety that was building somewhere inside me and nodded dumbly. I was sure it was a bad idea with my complete lack of censor today, but I figured that as long as I kept my mouth shut I'd be fine.

At the door I pulled my keys from my purse and smiled awkwardly at David. "Well, thanks. That was fun," I said quickly, making it clear I just wanted to get inside and away from all of this confusion.

"No problem. We'll have to do it again," he said smoothly. I swiftly put the keys in the lock and turned them, hearing the click as the deadbolt slid back. I turned back to David to give him a little wave when he suddenly slid his arms around my waist and pulled me against him. The utter shock on my face didn't seem to deter him at all. He was set on a purpose, and nothing was going to interfere, not even my clumsy half-formed question.

"David, what—?" I began, before he pressed his lips firmly against mine. I inhaled sharply, not quite sure how to react to this. For all of the relationships I'd been involved in ending, I'd never actually been in one myself, and it struck me in this moment that this was my first kiss. I felt a little pathetic, but I let that feeling slip away quickly and simply enjoyed everything about it—his warm breath against my lips as he pulled me closer to him, the way his hand rested on the small of my back, the soft pressure of his nose nudging my cheek with each persuasive kiss.

When he finally pulled back after what had to be nearly five minutes, I realized that my arms were circled around his neck. When had that happened? Embarrassed, I pulled them away and looked at the ground. What were you supposed to say after your first kiss? Thank you? That seemed a bit lame, but I didn't know what else I was supposed to do to break the silence. Did I just walk right into my house without a word? Maybe just a friendly reminder to call Claire? And tell her what? That he'd just kissed Amelia Bedford, the amazing breakup artist? I finally dared to look up at David and found acute confusion lining his features. Well, that couldn't be a good sign. There really wasn't a whole lot confusing about kissing. It was a pretty basic thing. I mean, even I had done pretty well for my first time, I'd say.

"I'm going to go now," he said distantly, distractedly. I nodded silently, afraid that if I spoke I'd ruin the moment even more than he was ruining it, which would be quite a feat. It only took seconds for him to get into his car and drive away, and I stood on my front porch, completely shaken.

I had just had my first kiss. And it wasn't a little peck of a first kiss. It was a major, earthshaking, intense, passionate first kiss. With a client. I turned that thought over in my head for a while, trying to decide what exactly that meant. I definitely had to give the money back, because there was no way things were going to work out now that I'd seduced the client. Or was it the other way around? I was pretty sure the client had just seduced me. I wasn't the one who threw myself into the kiss in the first place.

I sighed deeply, not even wanting to think of the mess I'd just gotten myself into. My brow was creased with anxiety as I made my way to my bedroom. I shouldn't have been so stupid. I'd never let a client walk me to the door before, because that only led to bad things, like kissing your impossibly cute paycheck. Ugh. What was wrong with me? I'd broken up with cuter boys for people before, but as much as I wanted to think it was just his looks that interested me, I knew it wasn't true. There were a lot of little things, even after the short amount of time I'd spent with him. It was the way he always raised his right eyebrow at me when I said weird things or the way only half of his mouth curved into a smile when he was trying not to make me feel uncomfortable.

But then again, there were a few red flags that I had been purposefully ignoring. He had asked some pointed questions that suggested he knew exactly what I was up to. Of course, that had to be crazy talk. He couldn't possibly know what I did for a living. My clients were all sworn to secrecy, not so much out of loyalty to me, but more out of an unspoken knowledge that if they told someone about my secret they'd have to start fighting their own battles because my business would be no more. So it had to be sheer paranoia talking. He had no idea what I did. He was just another boy I'd lured in with my good looks, and this time my pre-prom loneliness had gotten the better of me. I'd just have to work on controlling my emotions better in the future. Besides, now that I'd failed one client, at least I wouldn't have my perfect record hanging over my head. It wouldn't be such a shock on the day I failed another client. It was like never missing a day of school and then suddenly getting the flu. It was a situation completely out of my control, so I should just try not to fret over it.

I told myself that same explanation over and over again that night, and I eventually fell asleep, filled with an acute sadness that I couldn't quite seem to place. I ignored my thoughts of David and resolved to make it right on Monday. I'd straighten things out with Claire and give her the money back. Then I'd finish up my jock client and things could go back to normal. Perfect plan.

eleven

Sunday passed relatively uneventfully, though my mother did ask me how my date was. I quickly skirted the subject by just saying it was okay. She seemed to accept that response easily as she rushed out the door to work. She had started working Saturdays a few months ago and had recently added Sunday to her schedule. Her constant absence from the house was beginning to make me wonder if she was really going to work, or even going on dates. It seemed more likely that she had developed an entirely new family and I was the one she was sneaking away to see. She didn't have to work on Sundays because we certainly didn't need the money. I mean, we didn't have tons of cash stored away, but we had enough to be comfortable.

By Monday morning I had mentally prepared myself to break the news to Claire. I figured I'd leave out the hairy details and just tell her I wasn't able to finish the job. I had her fifty dollars stowed safely in my wallet, which rested in the white leather purse I'd tossed into the car. Driving in the hot pink high heels proved to be quite a challenge, but it was sure to be nothing compared to facing Claire. I only had to hope that Claire's ego wasn't hurt so badly that she would expose my line of work to the entire school. Not only would that ruin me, but she would be stupidly sabotaging her own personal protection against the awkwardness of breaking up in the future.

I stepped out of my car when I got to school and adjusted my bubblegum pink tank top so that it highlighted my assets. I counted on Blane's disposal to be easy, but I didn't want to take any chances with my newly shaken resolve. I turned around to grab my purse out of the car and caught my reflection in the window. My blonde hair was curly, and my makeup was expertly applied. Everything about me today said "look at me," which was completely opposite of the car I was staring into. My silver 1999 Hyundai Accent was about as inconspicuous as they come. I'd figured that I'd need something generic when I bought it, and so far it hadn't failed me. That and the car was reliable, so I didn't have to worry about breaking down in it, which was probably good, because if I did break down, no one would notice my car long enough to stop and help me.

The school was teeming with pre-prom excitement today. We only had two weeks until the blessed event, and everyone was already pairing off with unusual haste. I could see the lack of interest in the eyes of the couples, but their fear of being alone for something so big kept them glued to each other as if they were a vital part of life. I kept my jaw firmly set, trying not to scowl at the people around me, especially since I was receiving so many scowls from girls as it was. It had to be the outfit, but a lot of the girls in the school knew what I did, so they couldn't truly be mad at me for doing my job after they had all asked me to complete similar jobs many times before. I had gotten to school a little late that day, so I headed straight for psychology without looking for Claire.

I spent most of the class period reciting what I'd say to Claire in my head. I knew that I'd probably just forget my entire speech and throw the money at her before running away (which would be difficult in these heels) so the speech preparation was completely pointless. After class I headed to my locker only to find Claire there. Much to my surprise, she didn't seem angry. I'm guessing that meant she didn't know what I was about to tell her yet. This almost made it harder, having to spoil her good mood. When I approached she threw her arms around me with a knowing smile. I hugged her back awkwardly, wondering what I'd done to deserve such a warm welcome.

"Hey, Claire, I think we need to talk," I said stiffly, trying to keep the slight discomfort out of my voice.

"Yeah, we do. How on earth did you convince David to go back out with me? I mean, I have complete faith in you, Mia, I really do, but this was actually kind of shocking. Even for you. He was practically begging to have me back. It was wonderful. Now all I have to do is dump him at lunch in front of our friends and all will be forgiven." She smiled brightly at me, and I stared back at her, completely at a loss for words. After a moment of my open-mouthed gaping, I blinked.

"Oh. Right. No problem." I had absolutely no idea what was going on, but I smiled weakly at Claire as she bounded away down the hall. I still didn't understand her logic of breaking up with him in front of her friends. My job was to make it so that she didn't have to break up with him her-self . . . like I said, some of my clients really just wanted me to set up a dramatic situation for them. They couldn't care less about actually avoiding the awkward breakup.

After her retreat I opened my locker and rested my head against the propped-open door, letting the cool metal chill my forehead. None of this made any sense. Why had David decided he wanted Claire back so badly, especially after he'd just kissed me? Was I really that bad at kissing? That obviously wasn't the reason; I mean, even if I was a bad kisser, I couldn't possibly be bad enough to drive him back into Claire's arms.

As I gathered myself together and went off in pursuit of Blane, a million emotions ran through me. I was happy I'd avoided the inevitable failure of Claire's request, relieved that I had apparently had something to do with it, and hurt that David had begged to have her back. They'd never seemed happy together, even before I'd stepped in to ruin things for them. But as much as I hated to admit it, this was for the best. I couldn't let myself get too attached to people when my job was to destroy their happiness. Breathing in deeply, I let the thoughts of David go, hoping that they wouldn't haunt me anymore.

Blane was sitting in a group filled with jocks, a cheerleader at the very center of their attention. I had assumed Lexi had told her friends what I'd be doing, so I could at least avoid dirty looks from them as I threw myself at Blane. Putting on a peppy smile, I walked over to the group, very aware that I only had seven minutes until the bell would ring. It wasn't hard to get Blane's attention at all and I thought I might be able to get out of this one without a date. His head turned when he noticed all of his friends taking in the sight of me. He looked me up and down appreciatively, almost hungrily, and I suppressed an annoyed sigh.

"What can I do for you?" he asked, puckering his lips slightly as he waited for my response. Jocks were always so hard to deal with. Smile still firmly in place, I didn't answer and simply took a seat next to him. His friends watched me with disbelief, wondering why this hot girl had suddenly decided to infiltrate the ranks of the popular. The girls, however, jumped right back into conversation with their respective boyfriends, obviously in on what I was there for. With the focus of the group off of me, it was easier to concentrate on Blane, and just how to get rid of him.

I crossed my legs toward him so that my foot lightly rested against his calf. The skirt I was wearing was just short enough that it slid up slightly with this movement, instantly drawing Blane's eyes to my nicely tanned legs. I never really appreciated being ogled, but sometimes it was just the quickest way to get the job done. Obviously the flattering elements of my tank top weren't lost on him either as I launched into my story.

"My name's Amy," I said sweetly. "I'm friends with Lexi." These words brought a slight frown to his face as he remembered his girlfriend. I leaned a little closer to him as if to say that he could have me if only he didn't have that one little obstacle in the way. With that idea planted in his mind, I continued. "You see, she was sick today and we were supposed to hang out, so I figured, being the nice guy you are, you wouldn't mind if I sat with you?" I looked up at him from under my eyelashes, my face the perfect mask of innocence.

He smiled back at me and nodded. "Of course you can sit here," he said smoothly, obviously used to being approached by pretty girls. "And Lexi's not my girlfriend," he corrected me. Unlike the little situation with David and Claire, I knew for a fact that Lexi Monroe was still this boy's girlfriend, which meant the lie signified my partial success.

"Oh, well, that's funny," I said, still keeping my voice as guiltless as a child's, "because I thought you two were dating. She did actually seem to think it'd be a good idea if you guys maybe did break up though . . . which I must admit would make me pretty happy."

"She said that?" he asked, and for a moment I thought

I'd actually hurt his feelings. Silly me. "Well, that's a relief."
He breathed out a huge breath just to solidify his statement,
and I painfully kept my smile in place. This job had begun
to make me doubt relationships as a whole. It seemed like
almost everyone I had to break up was more than willing
to drop any connection they had with each other because of
popularity, or another pretty girl hitting on them, or their
stupid reputation. The whole thing seemed to be so messed
up and skewed from what reality should be. It was just sad.
And yet, here I was, making money off of the madness. I
didn't have time to ponder this though, because I felt the
presence of another body next to me instantly.

I looked over at the newcomer only to see David's grinning face staring back at me. "Hey, babe," he said, as if he'd
been saying it his whole life. I noticed with one quick visual
sweep that he was dressed differently today. He looked kind
of like a jock actually. Dressed almost exactly like Blane. My
eyes widened, and I quickly looked back to Blane, hoping
beyond all hope that if I just ignored him he'd go away. I didn't
quite know what he was doing, but it was bad whatever it was.

"Why are you over here instead of with me, where I can
appreciate the view a bit better?" He wrapped an arm around
my shoulder as he said this and nudged his nose against my
ear, sending instant shivers down my spine, which I point-
edly ignored.

"Is this your boyfriend?" Blane asked stupidly, obviously
a little slow on the uptake. This whole thing was going horribly wrong. I opened my mouth to say no, but amazingly
David beat me to it, informing Blane that he was, in fact, my
boyfriend. I turned around to face David, either so I could kill
him or yell at him, but when I turned he kissed me fiercely,
silencing my protests and solidifying his point to Blane.

"See ya," he said to the jock next to me as he ushered me

away, his arm still wrapped tightly around my shoulders. I was completely dumbstruck, my mouth hanging open slightly as he continued to push me through crowds of people. The bell had just rung, so the herd was moving quickly through the halls. David pulled me aside near a water fountain, which is when I finally regained my senses.

"What is wrong with you?" I whispered angrily. "I was . . ." I let my words trail off. I couldn't very well say I was working. That would give away my entire big secret.

"Yes?" he prompted a smug smile on his face.

"I was busy," I finished, keeping the anger hot in my voice. "Besides, Claire told me you two were back together," I spat, not needing to fake rage this time.

"Only until she breaks up with me at lunch," he said casually, as if this were the norm for a relationship, which, let's face it, in high school, it sort of is. I gaped at him, wondering how he knew this was what was going to happen. "Come on, Amelia, you didn't think I'd give up on you that easily, did you?" His words sent a slight panic through my whole body. He had figured it out.

"When did you find out?" I asked shakily. "Was it when I dyed my hair for no reason or when you saw me with Blane?" I was doing it again—the too-much-information thing. What if he didn't actually know anything and I was the one who'd just turned myself in?

"Give me some credit. Just because I'm dressed like a jock doesn't mean I think like one. I've known for well over a year, even with you changing schools all the time."

A year? How could he have possibly known for a year? As was often the case with David, nothing seemed to be making sense, but everything seemed to be falling apart. I took in a deep breath, aware of the quickly emptying hallway around us.

"So what do you want?" I asked finally.

"I want you to stop," he said simply. "It's not right. People need to fight their own battles. Besides, do you really think it's okay to break these boy's hearts and then make it seem okay with false promises?"

I made an indignant sound at him. He was being far too harsh. "All right, David, I don't know if you've noticed, but most of the relationships in high school aren't really true love, soul mate, eat your horrible cooking just because I love you type of things. They're 'I'll date you because it makes me look good and I'll dump you for the same reason.' That's what high school dating is all about, so I'm pretty sure I haven't ruined anyone's life." His assumptions were making me angry and the nonchalant way in which he judged me made me furious. Who was he to judge what I do?

"It doesn't matter if you're destroying people or not, Amelia. Don't you think you're hurting the people who hire you? If they never have to fight their own battles, isn't that a problem?" His voice held an angry edge that worried me, and I tried to grasp onto anything to defend my character with.

"You didn't even like Claire, did you?" I asked finally. He laughed a short, humorless laugh.

"She's one of your regular clients I've noticed, so I fig- ured I'd only have to date her for a week at the most in order to obtain the honor of meeting you." He said all of this with a wry smile on his face, and the expression made me want to slap him. Hard.

"So you used her to get to me. How is that any different than what you're preaching against? Apparently you're no angel, either."

"Do you really think I could hurt Claire by letting her date me for a week and then letting her break up with me?

I doubt she even remembers the names of half of her boy-friends." I knew that what he said was true but it definitely wasn't helping my case any. Why did I have to have such sleazy clients? It would be so much easier to defend my character if I actually had a weapon to defend it with.

"Why is it that you think the girls in this situation are horrible monsters and the boys are innocent angels being hurt by my acts?" So this was a slight exaggeration compared to what he had actually said, but he got my point.

"I'm not saying that, Amelia." Again with the chronic name usage. "I'm saying that both parties are victims of what you do. You're making it so that these girls don't learn how to do things for themselves, and you're obviously hurting the boys by denying them an actual explanation for their girlfriend's sudden cold feelings. Besides how do you know that your actions don't have more serious repercussions than what you actually see? Just because these boys don't break down in a fit of tears right in front of you doesn't mean that they aren't seriously hurting."

Being a person with no personality and no friends meant that no one questioned my judgment very often, which was exactly the way I liked things. It was difficult for me to stand by and listen to this boy make judgment calls about my character, when I might not even possess character. I glared at David for a moment before shaking my head.

"I'm going to be late for English," I said simply, storming off down the hallway.

"I'm really sorry, Amelia, but I'm going to have to end your business. But no hard feelings, okay?" I heard him call after me, answering the unspoken question I'd been too afraid to ask.

twelve

I spent all of English wondering if, despite David's interference, I'd been able to complete Lexi's assignment. Blane seemed to understand that they were officially broken up, but I didn't feel like I could be sure of anything anymore. When the bell finally rang for lunch, I stayed in my seat, unsure of what I should do. I knew what I definitely shouldn't do—I shouldn't go talk to Blane or David.

My only hope for any sanity this week was resting on Claire. If she really did break up with David during lunch, at least I'd be off the hook there. But what about David's threat to destroy my business? Could one boy really single-handedly tear down what I'd spent years building up? It didn't seem likely, but I couldn't keep a small, nagging feeling from penetrating my thoughts. David had, after all, been at this plan for at least a year. That small detail did rev up the paranoia quite a bit. That someone could actually be watching me for a year without my knowledge was extremely unsettling. I made it a point to blend in with the crowd and fade away at the right moment. I even went as far as to change schools often and convince my mom we should move around the valley to help her real estate business.

I shook these thoughts from my head long enough to realize that the classroom was empty and Mrs. Sanders was standing at the door, staring at me expectantly.

"Sorry," I mumbled to her as I slid through the door. She gave me the same worried look she always wore when I dyed my hair a different color or showed up to her class dressed in a completely different style. I ignored the look for now and slunk away from her class to go eat lunch by the library. I wasn't hungry, but I knew I had to eat something, so I took a bottle of water and a granola bar to my quiet little spot, away from everyone else. I passed all of the usual recluses on my way. Even though I'm sure they had begun to recognize me by now, they never said a word about my constantly shifting image. I smiled as I passed a small mousy girl with light brown hair. She always had her nose stuck in a book, but today I saw the corners of her eyes crinkle up into a smile as I passed.

I took my usual spot by myself and ripped open the shiny granola bar wrapper. Just looking at the thing made me feel sick to my stomach and so I just held onto it while I thought, letting my hands get sticky as my body temperature melted the sugary syrup. How had everything gotten so far off track so quickly? If it weren't for David and his little surprise attack, everything would be just fine.

"You're safe on both clients but this is the last time I can promise not to completely ruin everything," said an all-too-familiar voice. I looked up to see David staring down at me.

"Excuse me?" I asked, with as much venom in my voice as I could muster.

"Blane already has a new girlfriend, and Claire broke up with me a few minutes ago." I blinked up at him, trying to comprehend what he was saying. My clients had been taken care of, which meant that I hadn't failed, but this boy was still threatening to ruin my career. When I really looked closely at David to size up how much of a threat he posed, I noticed that he had completely changed. He was no longer wearing his jock attire, but a black T-shirt and jeans. Even his hair seemed to be a bit messier as it hung in his eyes. It was almost as if this boy were doing my job in exact reverse. He even dressed to fit the part he was playing.

So this whole thing was real. He knew where I came when I wasn't working. He knew that my wardrobe matched my clients'. He knew everything. So what had the date been about? Was he trying to get some great confession out of me? And had the purpose of the kiss been to simply make me doubt my career choice? Or maybe the kiss was just a perk for him for his year of hard work. I scowled at him now and stood up so we were almost equal, though he was a bit taller than me, even in the heels. I had to remember to keep my emotions under control. If he knew the kiss was still bothering me so much, then he would think he had won. He'd think he had some power over me. With this in mind, I pushed back any feelings that short, intimate experience had brought on and set my jaw stubbornly.

"Listen. I don't take kindly to threats. If you don't like my business, that's not my problem. And quite frankly, how I choose to make money is none of your business, so what gives you the right to come in here and screw with everything?" I felt like I'd burst into flames at any moment with the fiery heat of the anger I was feeling. At first my blow up had been about pride and fear of losing my job, but now that I had taken a moment to step back and really assess the situation, I could see that David was pulling rank where he had none.

"Amelia, the well-being of others is everyone's business," he answered calmly. What was he now, the guardian angel of high school flings? I'd had enough of this boy.

"Yeah, David, thanks for the infomercial, but I don't have to listen to this." I began walking away when he yelled out to me again.

"I don't want things to get messy. If you'll just stop this, I won't bother you anymore. But if you take on more clients I'll be forced to interject. Today was nothing," he added as an afterthought. I turned around and walked back to him, not quite ready to give up the fight yet.

"Why do you care so much? None of this has anything to do with you. I don't understand why you're making this into such a big deal. It's just high school." I stared at him, waiting for an answer because frankly, I was curious to know why a career choice that had nothing to do with him would be so offensive.

"Honestly?" he asked.

"Obviously," I answered snidely.

"I'd started hearing about you from friends. They had all been in the same situation and didn't realize until later that they had been dumped by proxy." He gave me a reproachful look here but I said nothing, so he went on. "Once I realized that all of these different people were talking about the same girl, I decided to track you down. At first I was offended for my friends that they hadn't been given an explanation for the relationship termination from the horse's mouth, but after I watched you for a while I became . . . fascinated."

His brows came together in a hard line and the same look of confusion that I'd seen on the doorstep returned. I gave a small shiver as flashbacks of Saturday night's little scene replayed in my mind. Yet again, I had to remind myself to focus.

"Why would someone dedicate their time in high school to doing the one thing people in high school are desperate to avoid? And then I thought that surely you were doing it for some outrageous price." I looked down at this, feeling a bit guilty that he knew I had been paid to break up with him. It must have been an awkward thing to find out.

"But fifty dollars, Amelia?" He sounded almost disappointed. "If you're going to be such a sleaze bag, at least charge more."

Whoa, I must have missed something in that conversation. I tried to quickly replay everything he'd just said but couldn't seem to find where he suddenly thought I was the one being ripped off.

"I thought you didn't like how I made money," I hurriedly pointed out.

"I don't like it or condone it in any way, but if you're going to sell your soul, at least make sure the devil isn't ripping you off." He said this all so matter-of-factly that I was beginning to wonder if he was actually a breakup artist also and he was just trying to scare me out of his territory. It wasn't so hard to believe.

"Anyway, we're digressing. What I'm trying to say is that I want to help you," he concluded, as if that statement made all the sense in the world.

"By destroying my one way of paying for college?" I asked sarcastically.

"Not your business. I want to burn your business to the ground. And I will. I want to help *you*." For some odd reason he thought putting the emphasis on different words made his point more clear. He might as well just emphasize every word for all the difference it made. I shook my head at him, showing that I still wasn't following whatever it was he was trying to say. He hesitated for a moment, which I found scary. Mr. Big Mouth didn't know how to put whatever it was he was trying to express into a fully formed sentence. "Are your parents still together?" he asked finally.

I let out a deep sigh of annoyance. So that's where this was going. He figured that I must be some poor, emotionally scarred girl who was so messed up inside that the only way she could comfort herself was by ruining other people's relationships. That had to make perfect sense, right? Because who would actually do my line of work if they weren't some kind of sadist?

"This has nothing to do with my parents," I said darkly, implying that he should simply drop it before I shoved my granola bar down his throat. He nodded his head slowly in a superior way that made me sick. He thought he'd really hit something now. I wondered secretly if he had some sort of timer going so that he could charge me by the minute for this psychology session. "My home life, like my job, is none of your business. So back off." I glared at him, my blue eyes burning holes into his green ones for as long as I could without blinking. He went longer. Of course. Anything that could possibly be annoying, this boy could do.

"Amelia, I want to help you get over whatever it is," he began, before I silenced him with a raise of my hand.

"I'm not a news story, David. I'm really sorry you need fuel for your writing, but it's not me." And with that I left for class, even though I still had a good ten minutes before the bell rang. I must admit though, the look of shock on his face as I walked away actually made the whole argument worth it. I had no idea why he was so surprised by my words, but honestly, right at that moment, I didn't care.

I knew David would probably try to follow me to class so I went the one place I could—the girl's bathroom. Once I was locked safely in a stall, I sat on the tank of the toilet and let my forehead rest on my knees as a hot tear slid down my cheek.

I'd been asked by many school counselors how I felt about

my father disappearing. Obviously it wasn't a big deal to me, but none of them seemed to believe that. They always told me it had to have some sort of deep psychological impact on my life that would manifest itself unconsciously in my actions, and I always waved away their suspicions with a laugh. Yet here David was, making—what I'm sure he thought—was a pretty obvious connection. A girl who ends relationships as a job must have divorced parents who don't have enough time to pay attention to her. This was simply a way of getting some attention. At least that's what he thought.

Of course I'd never ruled out the possibility that my odd choice in hobbies could have something to do with my father walking out on us, but it wasn't like I felt like a neglected child. I was fiercely independent and didn't need anyone else in my life telling me what I should do. It wasn't a hard concept to figure out, and yet people were always trying to analyze me and tell me how I felt. Shouldn't I know how I feel better than a complete stranger? There's nothing I hate more than people who think they know me because of one short interaction. In reality, there isn't a "me" to know. There's always only what the clients needed, and there's nothing more to my story.

Biology was the same as it ever was. We learned about things that were interesting but difficult to understand, which meant that half of the class was snoring within the first five minutes of lecture. I tapped my foot nervously all through the genetic code as my teacher pointed to different graphs and illustrations. I couldn't seem to focus all of my nervous energy. David had made it pretty clear that he planned on ruining my career if I kept taking on clients. That was a frightening prospect after the little demonstration of his effectiveness with Blane, though the fact that everything seemed to work out fine with Blane did give me some hope. The breakup actually seemed to go better after David's interference. Not only was I able to lure Blane away from Lexi, but I didn't have to worry about him pursuing me now that he thought I had a boyfriend. If it weren't for David's stubborn insistence that I was a horrible person for breaking people up, we could've started a pretty effective business together.

I stored that thought away for later consideration, even though it was a moot point. What I really needed to focus on right now was how to get David off my back. I refused to transfer my business to another school just because of some irksome boy. No, this simply had to be handled delicately. Luckily for me I had finished up all of my clients, so I didn't need to worry about the threat too much for now. I'd just have to be worried once Valentine's Day rolled around, or, more specifically, the day after Valentine's Day.

Amazingly enough we hadn't been given any biology homework, and so, with my spirits slightly higher, I made my way to my locker to drop off my book. I figured David would be off ruining someone else's life with his self-righteous psychobabble, so I didn't need to worry about him popping out of any corners. This didn't stop paranoid thoughts from creeping into my mind, though. If it weren't for the long brown hair and obviously feminine figure looming near my locker, I would have run in the other direction, swearing it was David.

I approached cautiously, fully aware that this was probably a potential client, which meant that my new little stalker wouldn't be happy. I looked over my shoulder self-consciously, as if expecting to see him standing there, but there were no bright green eyes in the swarm of students rushing to get home and away from the watchful gaze of teachers. I approached the brunette, noting with a touch of annoyance that I'd be dying my hair for the third time in only three weeks.

"Hi," I said, forcing an anxious smile onto my face. The girl smiled back sweetly, her green eyes instantly reminding me of the source of my unease. "How can I help you?" I asked, slipping easily into my professional tone.

"I heard you . . . help people? With awkward situations?" Her voice was timid, and I got the feeling that this whole idea made her nervous. I definitely couldn't imagine this girl breaking up with anyone herself—she was just too nice. This meant I'd be helping her, so, despite what David thought, I was a good person.

"Yes, I break up with people," I said matter-of-factly, since I was pretty sure she could never spit the sentence out. "For a small fee," I added hastily. I didn't enjoy taking money from people, but I wasn't putting myself through this for fun. She blushed slightly at my words, a pronounced pink that I'd bet her boyfriend thought was adorable.

"Oh, of course. How much is it?" She was just so soft-spoken and polite, it almost hurt to tell her my fee. I thought it might break the glass bubble surrounding her.

"Fifty," I remarked with another look around to make sure David wasn't lurking in a corner. She balked a little at the price but quickly rearranged her expression into one of neutrality.

"That's fine. So how exactly do we do this?"

I exhaled, not wanting to deal with this when I was in such a state of panic. I pulled out a crumpled piece of paper and quickly scribbled my email address onto it. I thrust the paper at her, beginning to feel a bit impatient that I wasn't already in my car on my way home. Safe.

"Send me this boy's name, age, three points of interest, and the date you need the job finished by. I'll also need your contact information in case there are any questions I may have about the boy." I said this all quickly and stiffly, as if I had memorized it long ago and it was just something I recited from time to time. "Oh, and a picture so I know what he looks like." The girl nodded shyly and I looked her up and down, memorizing her style and mannerisms quickly so that I'd know exactly what I'd be working on for the next few days.

She wore khaki pants with brown tennis shoes and a light pink three-quarter sleeved shirt. Her long brown hair was curly and pinned back away from her face so that the curls could cascade down her back. Basically, she looked like she stayed home all day and baked brownies for fun, and then went out on Saturday night and gave them to the homeless. I wasn't quite sure how I was supposed to seduce someone and be sweet at the same time, but that was the challenge I'd have to face.

"What's your name?" I asked, realizing that through my little schpeel I'd never gotten any information about her. I was just so used to summing a person up based on their style.

"I'm Karen," she answered quietly. Her voice seemed so drained of confidence that I indulged in a Romeo and Juliet type of fantasy for a moment, thinking that she really loved her boyfriend but they had to break up because their families hated each other. Of course, that whole scenario was ridiculous, but it worked just for that moment.

"All right, Karen. If you'll just email me that information, I'll get started on your job right away." She nodded as she silently read the address I had given her.

"I'll get the money to you tomorrow. I don't have it on

me right now . . . if that's all right?" Normally I never took a job without getting the money first, but Karen didn't really strike me as the type to have me work for her and then make off without paying me, so I agreed and said my good-byes.

The parking lot was almost completely empty by the time I made it out there. Students, who generally moved about as fast as a skateboard through a room of gravel, managed to get themselves going at a pretty decent pace when it meant they'd be leaving school. I walked to my car with my eyes trained on the ground, hoping that if I didn't see David while walking out to my car, he wouldn't see me. It was perfectly possible that he had already gone home, and I held onto that possibility with all my might.

Of course, my hoping did nothing. I looked up to find a sandy blond lounging against my silver car with an intent look on his face. I rolled my eyes at his serious expression and approached the car. He was leaning against the back door, leaving my door free, so I took full advantage of this and went straight for the keyhole. I plunged the key in, hoping that I could simply outmaneuver him and get into the car before he could say anything. He grabbed my hand just as I turned the key, however, and stopped me from getting any further.

"Do you agree to my terms?" he asked suddenly, as if picking up a conversation we'd ended only a few seconds earlier.

"What terms?" I grumbled. He sighed, obviously exasperated by my short-term memory.

"I want you to stop this little 'business' of yours, and I want to help you."

"Well, those aren't really terms, David. Terms would be more like 'you stop your business and I'll give you a million dollars.' Now those are terms I'd agree to." He looked at me with his brows drawn together in deep concern, and I glared back. "Oh, stop being so dramatic! It's not such a big deal, all right! I'm not emotionally scarred, I'm not a bad person, and there's nothing wrong with how I make money. You're the one who needs help. What kind of person dedicates a year of his life to following some girl around? Now that's creepy."

"Amelia, I don't know why you won't just admit that this has something to do with your own insecurities and not so much to do with making money." His tone aggravated me. It said, "I know what I'm talking about and you don't." It was superior and I'd had enough of it.

"Of course it has to do with money. I don't do this for fun, David. I just need money for college. Why is that so hard for you to believe?" It didn't make sense that he couldn't see the simple answer when it was right in front of him. It was pretty obvious that I did this for money, but his constant insistence that this was something else just baffled me. And the fact that he had decided to make it any of his business was complete nonsense.

"You could make more money at an after-school job than you are with this. Plus, from what I've noticed, you probably waste most of the money you make on hair products and new clothes for your clients." The obviousness of this statement did strike me for a moment. But only for a moment. I clicked my teeth together and looked up to the sky as if asking for assistance from some greater source to help me deal with this menace.

Perhaps I could make more at an after-school job, but if I did that, I wouldn't have an excuse to constantly change myself. I'd be a normal person set to the normal rules everyone else had to live by. I'd be expected to make friends and uphold relationships. I'd be expected to participate in the normal high school rituals like prom. And worst of all, I'd be expected to fit in with the rest of the crowd. I wouldn't fit in by choice, like I did when I pretended to be other people for my clients, but I would fit in because I'd be just like everyone else.

Though the money was definitely a perk, I couldn't deny that I enjoyed living by a different set of rules than my peers. It made me feel different and special to be able to stand back and criticize high school life without actually having to participate in it. I actually worried that if I had to start being a normal high school student I'd become so used to the mediocrity that I wouldn't even notice how normal I'd become. I'd just keep sinking into the crowd until I was as faceless as everyone else. I'd be given a brand like "jock," or "drama geek," or "nerd," and that would be that. No one would look past my label, or even have a desire to. They'd sum me up by what I wore or who I hung out with . . . just like I did with them.

The sad reality of this existence must have manifested itself on my face because David looked instantly concerned.

"Are you all right?" he asked, worry lining his features. I nodded silently and composed myself.

"I need to get home. My mom and I are going out to dinner," I lied. He nodded in understanding, still staring at me with acute concern, but he let me pass. Once in the car I drove to the store to get brown hair dye, and then home to my empty house. Once I got there I pulled some leftover chicken from the fridge. My mom hadn't bothered to leave a note this time, but I knew she wouldn't be home, so I finished my food, dyed my hair, and went to bed.

thirteen

I got up early the next morning to check my e-mail. Sure enough in my inbox there was one new message from Karen. I typed her information onto a fact sheet and printed it out. The sheet read:

Name—Nate
Age—16
POI—Gaming, geology, hiking
Deadline—ASAP

I wasn't quite sure why Karen hadn't given me a more specific deadline, but I could work with it, so I didn't complain. Looking in the mirror I was almost shocked when I saw my brown hair. No matter how many times I dyed my hair, that first look in the mirror was always a bit frightening. I combed my fingers through it, noting with pleasure that it was still soft and shiny. I was definitely blessed with resilient hair.

Opening up my closet, I browsed through it for some "nice girl" clothes and decided on some white Capri pants, a light blue short sleeved shirt, and white tennis shoes. I pulled half of my brown hair into a ponytail, letting the rest hang down with a small wave. Though I wasn't actually breaking up with the boy today, I wanted to get into character so I'd be more comfortable when I did it. I'd have to catch up with Karen at school today and orchestrate her upcoming "sick" day. Until then, I'd just hang back in the shadows and maybe observe her with Nate so I could get a better idea of what kind of boy I was dealing with.

As I pulled into the school parking lot, the silent threat David posed still hung in the air. I glanced around the area, doing a quick scan to make sure he wasn't nearby. When I was satisfied that he was nowhere to be found, I made my way to Karen's normal hangout. She had said that she and Nate were usually in the cafeteria between classes, so that was where I set my course.

The cafeteria was relatively empty, which didn't surprise me since most students ate breakfast at home or simply skipped the meal altogether. A few students huddled in close groups at the long picnic tables, exchanging that morning's gossip. Others sat alone, slouched over their miniature milk cartons with dazed looks on their faces.

I spotted Nate and Karen instantly. Today Karen's long brown hair was pulled up into a ponytail secured by a pale yellow ribbon. She laughed loudly at something Nate had said, but instantly slapped a hand over her mouth to stifle the sound. Her eyes grew wide and she giggled soundlessly at her own candid show of amusement. I smiled at her behavior in spite of myself. I looked over to survey the other half of the couple, which is when I saw Nate for the first time. He had short, light brown hair and the rosiest cheeks I had ever seen. His features, however, weren't what struck me about him. It was the look in his eyes that really stood out. The way he looked at Karen reminded me briefly of the way movie stars look at each other in romantic films, though this look was less polished. It was a warm, sincere look that could have melted anyone's heart. From where I stood, it actually appeared that Nate cared about Karen, rather than what she could do for his popularity or what she looked like. He actually looked into her eyes when she whispered things to him, and his smile was genuine.

It was a touching moment, but it was, sadly, completely irrelevant to what I had to do there. I sat down at an empty table near the door and took a plastic-wrapped bagel from my white backpack. I opened up my breakfast as quietly as I could, not wanting to draw any attention to myself. We only had about ten minutes before the first bell rang, warning us to get to class, so I decided to take those ten minutes to really observe the couple before me. Something about the entire situation didn't make sense. It didn't match up with the other clients I had helped before. Karen didn't look politely bored or audaciously interested in another boy; she looked happy. The blush I'd seen the day before returned to her cheeks at something Nate had said, and a smile spread across his face at the sight of her quickly reddening cheeks. Unless Karen was a wonderful actress, she was happy with Nate, and I was pretty sure she wouldn't be getting an Academy Award any time soon.

"You're doing another job," came a matter-of-fact voice beside me. I turned, my face set in grim annoyance, as I instantly recognized the voice.

"How do you pop up everywhere? Do you just dedicate your time to following me around?" I was angry at my break in concentration, and my voice showed it. David's eyes held mild amusement at my disgruntled expression.

"Actually, I just got lucky on this one. I always eat breakfast in here." He looked like he was trying to hold back his laughter at this fortuitous chain of events. "So, can I eat breakfast with you?" he asked finally. I shook my head firmly at his question and rose to leave, though his hand instantly encircled my wrist. "Please, Amelia?" Again I shook my head, though I did sit back down, against my better judgment. "What if I promise not to talk about our little disagreement at all? It'll just be a nice normal breakfast." Much to my surprise, his eyes actually looked hopeful, as if he really wanted to eat breakfast with me. I knew it was a bad idea, and every cell in my brain was telling me to leave, but my muscles didn't seem to listen to my brain, so there I sat. Fraternizing with the enemy.

David relaxed once he decided I wasn't going to leave, and he let a smile grace his lips. He pulled a granola bar out of his backpack along with a plastic bottle of orange juice. I picked at my bagel with a doleful expression on my face, hoping he'd take the hint. Karen and Nate were still giggling and whispering at their table, though now it only annoyed me, where seconds before I'd found it heartwarming. David looked at me sideways and laughed softly.

"Sitting with me isn't that bad, is it?" he asked with a grin. I turned my head to him, giving him a very clear look that answered his question in a second. He raised his eyebrows at me, still smirking, and shook his head. "All right, time to change the subject. How was dinner with your mom last night?" I looked down at my half eaten bagel, hoping to hide any hint of the truth my expression may show.

"It was fun. We did dinner and a movie. Probably stayed up later than we should have but it was worth it." I wasn't sure why I was lying since he'd probably bugged my house or something and knew that I'd really spent the evening eating reheated leftovers. If he detected the edge to my voice, however, he didn't show it.

"That sounds like fun," he said simply, without a smidgeon of sarcasm. I nodded my head but said nothing in response. Our conversation had definitely taken a turn for the awkward. I couldn't quite understand why David had decided to eat breakfast with me. It seemed odd that he was so bent on destroying me and yet he wanted to spend time with me. I suppose he could be trying to get to know me better so that it would be easier to take me down. After all, that's what I did to my customer's boyfriends. I sighed deeply, instantly attracting David's attention. "You all right?" He asked that question a lot.

"I guess," I said glumly. David always seemed to make me so depressed. It was a mixture between my hate for him and his stupid ideologies and my secret wish that he'd just realize that he wanted to be with me for the rest of his life so we could live happily ever after. "I feel like the victim of a kidnapping," I said suddenly, once again using my brilliant social skills around this boy who seemed to always make me say the most ridiculous things. David looked at me the way I expected him to—like he had no idea where that had come from.

"Why's that?" he asked.

"It's like you're holding my business hostage, and yet I'm forced to be around you and eat breakfast with you . . . so it's like you've kidnapped me, and even though I know you're trying to ruin my life, I have to be around you and treat you civilly." The words came spilling out of my mouth with absolutely no censor. I wasn't even sure if they made sense, but the whole thought process had definitely made sense in my head before it had made its big debut out of my mouth. Surprisingly David didn't look confused, but disappointed.

"Maybe you'll get Stockholm Syndrome," he said with a laugh before turning serious again. "Amelia, I know you feel

like I'm ruining your life or sticking my nose in your business, but I'm really trying to help you. I'm sure I sound like
a shrink or something, but you really do fascinate me." He
stopped short once those words left his mouth and I wondered if he was rethinking what he'd said or just wondering
if he'd come off as a creepy stalker. I was still bothered by
his insistence that he belonged in my life somehow, but I
couldn't help but feel a small twinge of affection for him. He
kept his gaze trained on me expectantly and I looked around
for some kind of out. Karen and Nate had left without me
noticing, so I took this as the perfect opportunity.

"I need to go. I've lost track of my client." I stood from
the table, leaving my bagel behind and walked away from
the cafeteria, feeling the oddest impulse to turn around and
go back to where David sat with a frustrated expression on
his face. I instantly heard footsteps behind me, which I knew
were David's so I turned abruptly to thwart any attempt he
was making to follow me. "What do you want? Why can't
you just leave me alone?"

"Because I'm—"

"Trying to help me? Yeah, I know, you've used that line.
What is it you really want? You know there's nothing morally wrong with my business. If people want me to help them
break up with their boyfriends, that's between them and me.
It has nothing to do with you, so just stay out of it. Besides,
you can't do anything to stop me. You don't have some claim
over the hearts of angsty high school boys." I glared up at
the guy who stood before me. His shaggy blond hair was
hanging in his green eyes as usual, and the glare he wore
matched mine perfectly.

"You're not doing anyone any favors by doing this. They
should do this on their own. It's not like they'll be able to
hire someone to take their tests for them or grieve at their

parent's graves when that time comes. You're really hurting people and you don't even see it. If you could just see how much these meaningless little high school relationships mean to some people, I don't think you'd be so bent on destroying them." A look of sadness passed over his handsome features, catching me completely off guard. This look lasted only a moment though before it hardened and he continued on his tirade. "Life is hard. Sometimes we have to do stuff that sucks. That's just the way it is."

"All the more reason for me to make one less thing a burden, don't you think? Besides, if you're worried about me being the cause of heartbreak, you can just shelf that theory. These couples would break up anyway. I'm just speeding the process along a little."

"That's not what bothers me!" he shouted, and I was instantly glad that the cafeteria was almost empty so that we only had to endure a few curiously aggravated stares.

"Well then, what is it, David? Did your friends' breakups really bother you that much? Apparently you're the one who needs to learn to deal with hardship, not my clients." I did feel a bit bad about the words that were escaping my mouth especially since he got that same "you just ran over my dog" look that he had given me on our date. I was a generally pleasant person. I couldn't remember a time I'd ever raised my voice at someone, but for some reason David just had a special way of getting under my skin. David looked at me intently, biting his bottom lip to keep from swearing at me, I'm assuming. He took a deep breath and closed his eyes for a moment before speaking.

"At first I was really bothered by what happened to my friends. I guess I still am in a roundabout way." His tone was even again, and the stares that had been trained on us were now back on their food. "I was really angry that their girlfriends hadn't had enough decency to at least break things off themselves. It still would have been hard for them to hear about the demise of their relationships but when they're set up to look like something they're not . . ." His words trailed off then. Quite possibly because he realized that I had absolutely no idea what he was talking about. It was like we had been reading a book and thirty pages had been cut out of my copy. Shaking his head and apparently deciding to give up on whatever direction he was taking with this little talk he continued, "That's when I decided to ruin your career. But like I said, I became fascinated by what you do. Well . . . why you do it, really. And then, when I went in for the kill to topple your carefully practiced business, I made a mistake." He looked at the ground now, some of his confidence obviously leaving him. It was odd to see David looking shy when he'd always seemed so outgoing and forward to me.

I kept my eyes locked on him, waiting for him to reveal what the mistake was. I saw a small blush rise in his cheeks and I immediately knew: he had kissed me. He'd gotten attached to his work just like I had that night. It was really an easy problem to resolve—we would simply stay out of each other's way and it would all be forgotten. But we didn't seem able to do that.

"So you don't want me to stop my business out of some moral obligation?" I said quietly, though I was pretty sure I already knew the answer. He shook his head, raising his eyes slowly until they met mine. He almost looked embarrassed and I wondered, in a moment of chagrin, if he'd ever had to ask a girl to be interested in him. Not that I wasn't interested in him already. But the mere fact that he actually needed to ask me to choose him over something else was apparently more than he'd had to do in the past.

The bell rang, causing us both to jump, and I looked

around the cafeteria to see that it was already empty. I looked back to the boy who stood in front of me, the one boy who'd ever been interested in the real me, the me I didn't even know existed. And of course, I did the exact opposite of what I knew I should have done. I walked away without saying another word.

I have absolutely no idea what we talked about in history that day. My thoughts were completely consumed with David's sudden interest in me. Well, I guess it wasn't so sudden if he'd been dwelling on this for a year. But that confused me even more than if it had been sudden. That meant this boy had been thinking about me for a year and still wasn't bored by the concept of me. Most of my clients got bored with their significant others after a week. I wasn't sure I'd ever seen someone stay together for a whole year. The mere idea was almost too much for my brain to handle.

I rubbed at my temples with my eyes closed. I hadn't even realized that the teacher had popped in a DVD until I felt a light tap on my shoulder. Opening my eyes, I glanced up at Mrs. Recht. She stood at a mere 4'11" at full height and her short brown hair bounced when she walked. Her thick black-rimmed glasses always seemed chic to me; they didn't match the rest of her wardrobe at all. The muted neutral skirts and tucked-in white blouses seemed like something straight out of one of her ancient archaeology videos. I gave her a wary smile, sure I was about to get in trouble for not listening to the lecture.

"Amelia, are you feeling all right?" she asked with genuine concern. I'm sure she didn't want the truth, which was that I felt like jumping off a cliff. There was no need to cause any undue panic, so I simply shook my head. She nodded in response. "I didn't think so. Would you like to go to the nurse?"

"Yes, please," I whispered, glad she had waited until she started the movie to talk to me, rather than singling me out during her lecture. The last thing I wanted was people staring at me any more than they normally did. Mrs. Recht scribbled down a note and her signature on a yellow slip and handed it to me.

"Feel better, dear," she said with more motherly concern than I'd ever even heard from my own mother. I smiled at her, instantly thankful for all concerned teachers who were actually invested in the well-being of their students.

Trekking to the nurse's office, I went over my speech in my head. I just have a really bad headache and can't concentrate on class right now. Can I go home? That sounded believable enough, though I didn't know if the nurse actually sent people home for headaches. I'd never been in the nurse's office before, which seemed a bit odd. I guess I really had missed out on everything having to do with the normal high school experience.

Why was that? Why couldn't I have a normal relationship with a person? Wasn't that more important than utilizing my God-given skills? And wasn't David right in saying that I could make more money at a less entertaining but much easier after-school job? Looking back on my total relationships, not just romantic, but human in general, I couldn't count one that had actually lasted. I had my one friend in elementary school and I had my mother. My mother and I barely even spoke once my father left. She always found ways to keep herself busy, and I seriously suspected that she had another family she wasn't telling me about. I practically lived alone. Even when I was at school and surrounded by people, I was still alone. I didn't have any friends or any boyfriends, and I didn't talk to anyone in my family. How could someone live their entire life without human contact?

Perhaps I expected things to get better once I started college. Like, if I could just hold on until then I'd suddenly find a million people who'd want to hang out with me and a perfect boyfriend who'd like me for who I was . . . like David seemed to. It was a frightening thought, but I really did have two choices at the moment: I could continue on in my normal pattern, being comfortably aloof and separate from the normal world of human relationships, or I could quit my job and be with David at the risk of actually connecting with another person. It seemed like the answer should be obvious, but if I gave up my job I'd be giving up the only constant in my life. The only thing that had stayed with me forever wasn't a person, but a hobby. People were unpredictable and flaky, but my hobby, which I was in control of and governed, was always there for me. As dumb as it sounded, giving up my job would be like giving up my only friend. It had almost become an addiction or a comfort blanket for me. But perhaps that was one of the big reasons I should drop it now, before it became such a crutch that I'd never be able to stand on my own without it.

"Are you all right?" came a voice from in front of me. I blinked away my thoughts in confusion and looked down at the plump nurse behind the desk. Apparently I'd wandered over to her office without any awareness that I was doing so. I'm sure I had a dazed look on my face and I wondered how long I had been standing there, looking like a zombie.

"Excuse me?" I asked, not quite sure what she had said to me only moments before.

"I said, are you all right?" She looked slightly frightened

now, as if I would suddenly slip into a coma and her medical training would be truly tested.

"Oh yeah, I'm fine. I think I just need to lie down for a minute. Am I allowed to do that here?" My question had genuinely thrown her off balance. She eyed me with incredulity, though I had no idea why my request had seemed so outrageous. She pried her eyes away from me and began typing on her computer.

"Name?" she asked mechanically.

"Amelia Marie Bedford," I recited, still dwelling on my options for my future. She clicked away on the keyboard, then looked up at me suspiciously.

"You're sixteen?" she asked, as if I might lie about my age. I thought women only did that when they turned thirty.

"Yes," I said, equally as suspicious of where she was going with this.

"You're a sophomore?" I simply nodded my head this time, wondering why she was asking questions with such obvious answers. "And you've never been to the nurse's office?" Ah. Now I knew where the suspicion was coming from.

"I don't get sick very often," I said, figuring that would clear things up. The woman looked me up and down for a minute. I'm assuming she decided that if I hadn't faked a headache in my whole high school and junior high career, I probably wouldn't start now.

"You can go ahead and lie on that bed there," she finally said, pointing to something that I thought looked nothing like a bed. It was more like a long brown armrest with wax paper over it. "Would you like something for your head?" she asked, her tone much more hospitable now that she knew I wasn't one of those students who came to the nurse's office every day because they mysteriously developed a headache during P.E. and math.

"No, I think I'll be fine. I just need to rest for a moment," I answered, keeping my tone sweet and believable. The truth was that I just needed time to think about what I was going to do with the new choices in front of me. I lay down on the "bed," which made funny crinkling sounds when the wax paper stuff bent under my weight. I wondered if they just threw the paper away after someone sat on it. Surely the school wouldn't waste paper like that when hundreds of sick kids have sat at my classroom desk. Nobody threw those away after every use.

I let that tangent go, deciding to focus on the problems at hand. With my eyes closed and my arm resting lightly over my forehead, I went back over my options. Option 1: stay alone but quite within my comfort zone for the rest of my life. Option 2: drop my job, sink to everyone else's level, and date a truly gorgeous and interesting boy. I guess saying that I'd be sinking to everyone else's level was a bit arrogant of me. It wasn't like I was above everyone else . . . I had just always thought of myself as separate from them, so to be just another part of the crowd was a less-than-desirable idea. However, I could comfort myself by thinking that if my only contact with the normal high school world was through a boyfriend, I still wasn't really participating in the ridiculous high school stereotypes and primitive courting rituals. I could still maintain my individuality without being completely cut off. This could actually work.

With a smile slowly spreading across my face and a plan fully formed in my mind, I waited for the bell to ring so that I could set everything in motion.

fourteen

I scanned the crowd during break, a nervous anticipation growing in my stomach. This was the first time since I'd met David that I was looking for him because I wanted to talk to him, rather than trying to avoid him like the plague. I half expected him to just pop up behind me like he always did, but perhaps I'd hurt his ego during our last encounter. Trying to ignore that possibility, I walked through the quad and over to my spot near the library, hoping he might be waiting for me there. The spot, however, was empty, just waiting to absorb the girl who had no friends and no family. I looked glumly at the empty wall before sliding to my normal place on the ground and resting my head on my knees. I was wearing white pants, so this probably wasn't the best place to sit, but I had far more important things on my mind at the moment. Perhaps I hadn't thought my brilliant plan through all the way. I hadn't anticipated the possibility that David might not want to talk to me now. After all, I couldn't expect him to wait around forever, though you'd think after waiting for a year, one class period wouldn't really break his spirit.

I vaguely registered the presence of a warm body sliding down to sit beside me and when the miraculous smell that belonged to David hit my nose, a grin plastered itself to my face. I looked up at him, noting that he didn't look particularly mad at me, just a bit resigned. "I wasn't going to bother you but you looked a little sad," he said dully. I could see his green eyes scanning my face, and when they took in the smile that I'm sure looked a bit maniacal, he smiled back tentatively. "So are you okay?"

"I'm wonderful," I replied happily. "At least I think I am . . . or I will be." He looked at me as if I were crazy, which seemed to be a normal expression for him, and I simply beamed back. "I think this could work," I said finally.

"Wait, this as in this?" He motioned to himself and then me, implying that I meant "us."

"Well, I was thinking about it, and maybe it wouldn't be so bad to actually talk to someone other than myself, and make plans with someone other than myself, and . . . oh that's right, actually have a friend other than myself." He smiled at this and scooted closer, apparently coming to the decision that I wasn't about to bite his head off.

"I'm glad you find me worthy to be in your presence, oh great one," he said dramatically. I shoved him in the shoulder but went on, undaunted by his sarcasm.

"I mean it. I actually like you. Despite the fact that you're self-righteous and frustrating, and you've been following me around for a year, which is pretty creepy—"

"Please don't flatter me, you're making me blush," he said in a monotone voice.

"The thing is the whole 'liking someone' thing?—that's never happened to me before. I've never wanted to be with someone. I've always been perfectly fine on my own, and then I met you and it was just . . . different." I realized I was ranting, which was something I always did, but it usually happened in my head so those around me didn't have to be subjected to it. Then again, that was David. He always made me say the strangest things—the kind of things that really belong in your head, that you always think but never say. Being around David was like taking some sort of honesty pill.

"I'm going to finish up with Nate and Karen and then I'm done. Those were your terms after all, weren't they?" I smiled at him, actually excited by this thrilling new prospect.

"They were," he agreed, still sounding a bit apprehensive of my motives. "Are you sure this is what you want? I mean, I don't want you to be unhappy, and I realize I've been making you pretty miserable this week." He looked down guiltily, though I could see a hint of a smile on his face. He didn't really feel all that bad.

Without bothering to vocally tell him that this was indeed what I wanted, I lifted his chin and leaned over and kissed him. It was a long, wonderful, blissful kiss that felt like it might just keep going until the bell rang, and when he finally pulled away, my arms had, yet again, encircled his neck somehow, which proved to be slightly uncomfortable since we were sitting down. It was odd how I had no idea what was going on when I kissed him. Instead, I just sort of lived for that moment. I was also beginning to notice that now that I'd kissed him once, I was becoming a bit of an addict. Under any other circumstances I'd never take the initiative and kiss a boy, even if we'd kissed before. I suppose that was all part of the new Amelia.

David brought his hand to my cheek and gave me one more small kiss before leaning his back against the wall once again. "I'll take that as a yes," he said breathlessly. He closed his eyes and smiled. "It's weird though." I raised an eyebrow at these words, not quite sure what to make of them.

"What's weird?" Surely he didn't mean my kissing. I really had to stop worrying about that. It's like I'd said before—it's a pretty basic thing. How bad could I be?

"Just the way all of this came about. I mean, I set out to destroy you, and then became a bit infatuated with you. You set out to ruin my fake relationship, and then you started to like me. We have to have the most screwed-up relationship in the history of all screwed-up high school relationships." He laughed quietly, his eyes still closed. I followed his example and leaned my head back against the wall, closing my eyes.

It was like a release from the craziness of the past week, just to sit there with David in silence, thinking about how we got to this point. I felt such a mix of emotions that it was almost difficult to catalogue them into separate categories just then. I was happy that I was actually going to make a connection with someone other than myself, I was scared out of my mind at the prospect of change and the unknown, and I was really wanting to kiss David again. Now that I had that option open on a consistent basis, I'd have to learn to keep my emotions under control. Except, now that he was my boyfriend, I should be able to kiss him whenever I wanted to. Or at least . . . I thought he was my boyfriend. I guess we hadn't actually had that talk.

"So . . . do we need a DTR or are we pretty much past that?" I asked, opening my eyes to look at him. He turned his head in my direction so he could take in my expression.

"Is DTR some relationship acronym that only breakup artists know about?" I quickly remembered that not everyone spoke the same language as I did for my line of work: DTR, POI, CF.

"It means Define the Relationship. It's that horribly awkward talk couples have when they aren't sure if they're a couple of not . . . it's basically a way to force someone into telling you if you're their girlfriend or boyfriend." I blushed slightly, never thinking I would stoop so low as to have a DTR. Those kinds of talks were for sappy high school students who actually thought their relationship would last through the whole week. It was slightly embarrassing that I had joined the ranks of the love struck, but there it was. The truth is sometimes painful to accept.

"Ah," he said mysteriously, a grin creeping onto his face. Sometimes David's lack of normal human responses was so frustrating.

"Well, glad we cleared that up," I said sarcastically. I was doing it again. I was desperate for him to tell me what we were. I actually cared if we had an official title of couple or not. The new me was so pathetic, and yet I loved it. He kept his grin in place and entwined his fingers with mine, giving my hand a little squeeze.

"I definitely think we're past that talk. I stalked you for a year and you hated me for trying to ruin your life . . . I'd say that makes us a couple, wouldn't you?" I laughed and nodded in agreement. "So, just one more job, right?" he asked. Oddly enough, the fact that this was kind of a possessive thing to say didn't bother me at all. It struck me as sweet. Oh yeah, I was disgustingly infatuated with him. It was odd how easy it was to confuse love and hate. Yesterday I wanted to blast him off the face of the earth and today I just wanted to be close to him and breathe in his intoxicating scent.

"One more. Nate and Karen," I confirmed. "I don't think it'll be that hard except that they seem to actually like each other . . . which doesn't make much sense." David looked at me with confusion lining his features but said nothing, apparently not wanting to get involved in the line of work he found so distasteful.

The bell rang then, signaling the end of break, and the

two of us stood. I looked around awkwardly for a moment, wondering what I was supposed to say to my new boyfriend. The whole fact that I was even wondering such a thing was a bit embarrassing, but I'd just have to live with my newfound sense of reality. Before I could decide what would be best, David slid his arms artfully around my waist, giving me chills all over. He pulled me close to him, his hands on the small of my back, and gave me one long, deep kiss. When he broke away I sighed, reminding me forcefully of some pitiable character in a romance novel. He smiled at this and said, "See you at lunch," before walking back through the quad to his class. And there I stood, left with a stupid grin on my face and obviously blushing cheeks.

My ASL class was actually interesting enough to keep my attention, though my mind was trying its hardest to be distracted. We learned the various signs for different food items and I decided I'd have to show David the sign for shrimp after class because it was just so comical. That thought made me smile. Having someone to share things with and someone to look forward to seeing was a first for me. It made me feel like I actually had a purpose or a reason for being here.

When class was over, I was the first one out the door, startling a few of my classmates as I pushed past them to get to my little spot by the library. When I got there, the wall was empty, which puzzled me for a moment, making me wonder if I had imagined the whole scene at break. I quickly realized, however, that it was, in fact, lunch, and David was probably getting food, which was something I had forgotten to do in my excitement. I slid down the wall and sat impatiently, scanning the passing students for David's bright green eyes. He was there only two minutes later, carrying two long, skinny items wrapped in foil. I refrained from jumping up and running over to him and decided to maintain at least a little dignity. He slid down next to me on the ground, and we both sat in silence for a moment.

"So . . . I'm not still a job or anything, am I?" he asked suddenly, catching me entirely off guard.

"I don't think I understand the question," I said honestly. Well . . . semi-honestly.

"Well, I just realized that all of this elation and 'Oh, I'm so happy to be in a relationship with this boy that I hate' stuff could really just be me falling into one of your expertly laid traps. I mean . . . you really, really don't like me. Remember?" He said all of this with the same infuriating smirk that he always wore.

"Well . . . if you were a job, I couldn't very well tell you now, could I?" I countered, trying to sound sly and unpredictable. It didn't work. "I'm starting to think that hating someone and really liking them are incredibly similar."

"So what you're telling me is that you feel like you probably like me . . . but at any moment you could realize you just want to push me down a flight of stairs? That sounds about like every healthy relationship I've ever seen," he said with a shrug, and I couldn't really tell if he was joking or not. It was a lot harder to read David than it was to read all the other boys I had broken up with over the years.

Looking at our current relationship, I had to admit that this was the scariest way possible to jump into having a normal life. I wanted so badly to believe that David and I had just gotten lucky to be that one-in-a-million exception to the short-lived, high school relationship rule. The worry that this was a superficial connection permeated my mind, but I pushed it back to pull out and examine at some other time.

"I brought you a lettuce wrap," he said, placing one of the foil items in my hand. "I know you like them . . . which makes me sound like a stalker."

"If the shoe fits," I answered with a shrug. We ate in silence for a moment and I let my gaze roam to the library entrance where Nate and Karen were talking right outside the door. I made a mental note to talk to Karen after school so that I could get the job done tomorrow. David followed my gaze to the conversing couple and raised an eyebrow.

"Is that them?" he asked casually, though I knew he was a bit uncomfortable with work talk. He'd just have to get over that for the next two days. It wasn't like I was a stripper or something; my work wasn't that difficult to talk about.

"Yeah." I continued looking at them. Karen seemed upset by something. Her face was flushed and her hand continually went up to her cheeks as if she were wiping away tears I couldn't see from this distance. Nate put his arm around her and kissed her forehead, quietly comforting his girlfriend. He didn't look around him to see who was watching this ordeal; he simply focused all of his attention on her. He really did care for her.

"Do you see that?" I asked after a moment of silence. "Do you see how he's not worried about if comforting a girl is scoring him brownie points with the other girls in the school or making him any less cool to the boys? He just doesn't care about that kind of stuff." I was thinking out loud again, but I thought maybe David could help me figure this mystery out. "They actually like each other," I said incredulously.

"That has been known to happen sometimes," David replied with a laugh. I was sure he thought I was some sort of hardened, unlovable freak show after my notorious career.

And yet he still wanted me. So maybe he was right—it has been known to happen.

"I can see that," I said, turning to him with a smile before returning to concentrate on the last job in my extensive career. "It's just . . . people who actually like each other are so infrequent. I never see them in my line of work. Why would two people who like each other want to break up?" None of it made sense.

"Maybe you should ask her." David suggested with such obviousness that I couldn't believe I hadn't thought about that before. I didn't say anything to this suggestion but nodded in agreement, trying to figure out exactly how I could approach the subject without seeming nosey.

"That's enough work for one lunch period," I said finally, returning my gaze to David. My boyfriend.

"So I was thinking that maybe we could try our first date over again. Now that you don't have to think of a good lie for every question I ask you." He was smirking but the mention of that night made me shake my head.

"You're horrible! You knew the whole time I was lying to you, didn't you?" I asked, though I was pretty sure I knew the answer.

"Why do you think I was so interested in your past? I wanted to see how good you were at thinking on your feet. I must say, now that you're looking for a new job, you should seriously consider acting." I shook my head at him, amazed that I had been the butt of his own personal joke without my knowledge.

"I think a second first date is definitely in order," I answered with a playful glare.

"How about Friday at about five?"

"Well, we both know my schedule is pretty free now," I said just as the bell rang. I wasn't sure how the time had flown by so quickly when I could have sworn that we had just sat down for lunch. We stood again and I threw our trash into the nearby can.

"Friday it is then," he answered, before repeating the scene at break and pulling me into him. I could smell what I was sure had to be some sort of cologne, and I put my arms around his neck, resting one hand on his soft blond hair. He placed his forehead lightly against mine and smiled. "I'm glad we got that cleared up," he whispered before kissing me once more. I was definitely an addict. Even though the occurrence was becoming more and more frequent, kissing David never ceased to make me feel dizzy. I knew there had to be some sort of social no-no about kissing in the middle of a crowded high school where everyone could see you, but I truly didn't care. David didn't seem to either, since our kisses were becoming longer and more involved every time they happened. When he pulled away to go to his last class, a thought struck me, and I grabbed his hand to stop him.

"Why did you take me out so late on our first date?" I asked, genuinely puzzled and curious. A grin crept across his face, making my heart skip a beat.

"I was pretty sure I would chicken out, and I just wanted to give you plenty of time to bail so I wouldn't have to," he said simply, and then he released my hand to go to class.

I shook my head with a smile, watching him go. At least I wasn't the only one who was out of my element.

Trying to pay any attention to my math class was simply out of the question. Not only did I not understand a word of what my teacher was saying, but I was too focused on my upcoming date and the little talk I needed to have with

Karen to concentrate on anything else. I tapped my pencil on my desk absentmindedly, playing the confrontation out in my head. Okay, so maybe confrontation wasn't the right word to use. It really wouldn't be too difficult; I simply had to ask why she wanted to break up with Nate when they seemed to be so completely attached at the hip. She didn't even seem to be faking her affection as some of my more kind clients would do to their soon-to-be ex-boyfriends. I went over the situation in my mind until it seemed like an abstract concept, and finally the bell rang.

I walked slowly to find Karen, feeling that this was a conversation I would need to have in person rather than on the phone. She was in one of the long hallways where a row of brown lockers stood. She had her back to me, and I felt a bit like a lion on some nature show, creeping up on my unsuspecting prey. I tapped her shoulder lightly and was met with a drained-looking Karen. Her face was pale and her eyes were red rimmed. Even her constantly blushing cheeks seemed completely lifeless and pallid.

"Karen, are you all right?" I asked automatically, true concern filling my voice. As a rule I never cared much about clients, and they never cared much about me. What I did was strictly business and that was how I liked to keep it, but Karen was such a sweet girl that I couldn't help but feel genuinely worried about her.

"I guess I won't have too much trouble faking sick tomorrow, huh? I didn't think I looked that bad," she answered, a joyless smile on her pale lips. "And I'm fine. I just don't feel well. I think I'm getting the flu or something." She shrugged this thought off and coughed into her hand before shutting her locker. I kept my eyes trained on her, afraid that if I let her escape my line of sight for a second she would just fall over right on the spot.

"Do you need help getting to your car?" I asked apprehensively.

"No, my mom picks me up. I'll be just fine." She began to walk away with a weak wave of her hand before I stopped her. I didn't want to stress her out when she was so obviously in pain, but I needed to know that she really wanted me to end her relationship tomorrow.

"I just have a quick question about the job tomorrow," I said as neutrally as I could. She nodded, urging me to continue, and obviously wanting to get home to rest. Her eyes looked so tired. "Are you sure you want me to do it? I mean, I've been watching you and Nate, and you two seem really happy together." I tried to keep my voice even and sound as uninterested as I could. Karen simply sighed and let her gaze fall to the ground.

"I really do love him," she said in a voice so resigned I wondered if my Romeo and Juliet theory was right after all. "I just can't be with him right now. It'd be better if we were just friends." She said all of this in a mechanical way, as if she had rehearsed the answer to this exact question in her mind so many times that saying it had become redundant.

"You love him?" I asked, registering that she sounded as if she meant it. I'd only heard a handful of my clients use the word *love*, and most of the time it was something more like "Well, Amelia, I need you to break up with him because there's this cute new exchange student that I just love." The word had lost its meaning to me, and I always thought of it as a cheap title for lust. The way it came from Karen's mouth, however, made me rethink that assessment.

"I really do," she answered, still sounding resigned. "It's just . . . well . . . my mom won't let me have a boyfriend. She's so overprotective and I know she does it because she loves me and she's worried, but that doesn't make it any easier,"

Karen's voice cracked slightly, and I could tell she was trying not to let her emotions get the better of her. "She said that if she found out I was dating someone, she'd start homeschooling me again." A single tear slid down Karen's ashen cheek, and she looked up at me with her big green eyes that looked so much like David's. "If I get taken out of school, I won't be able to see him at all. At least if we're broken up I can see him around school, even if it means I see him with another girl or completely over me." Her words had stunned me into silence. The Romeo and Juliet theory was just a musing in my mind—I hadn't thought Karen and Nate's relationship was actually some sort of forbidden romance. I tried to clear these thoughts from my head.

"Why don't you just tell your mom that you don't have a boyfriend but continue to see Nate?" I asked. I was pretty sure lying to your parents was not the kind of advice I should be dispensing, but it seemed to be a semi-desperate situation. Besides, no mother would dislike Nate, I was sure of it.

"I can't lie to my mother," she said with so much disgust in her voice that I instantly regretted my words. It was true that I never lied to my mother. I just stretched the truth a bit. But then again, my mother wasn't around enough for me to lie to her.

"Well, then how about just telling Nate exactly what you told me? I'm sure he'd understand if you let him know that you weren't breaking up with him because you wanted to."

"He wouldn't understand. He already knows my mom doesn't want me dating anyone, but if I broke up with him because of it, he'd just try to reason with me and talk me out of it." She looked at the ground again, looking more fragile than when I'd first walked up to meet her. "I'd see his side of the argument and stay with him. But that's not an option, so I need someone else to do it for me." Another tear trailed down her cheek. "It really is for the best," she added, more to herself than to me.

"If you're sure, Karen," I said sympathetically. I'd never run into this situation before. It just figured that the day I met someone who actually had a legitimate caring relationship, there would be no way for me to save it. Some marriage counselor I was going to be.

"I'm sure," she whispered. And with that she was gone.

fifteen

My mom wasn't home when I arrived from school, which didn't surprise me too much, though it was always a disappointment. I found some leftover steak and potatoes from one of her "client dinners," so I reheated it and made that my dinner. I spent that night trying to figure out how to woo Nate when I was supposed to be someone as sweet as Karen. After my little conversation with Karen earlier in the day, I had found David waiting by my car and had asked his advice on the situation, thinking he'd have a bit more insight than I did. Sadly, he couldn't think of an easy way around the whole mess, so we parted there with the promise that I'd see him the next day.

I was so exhausted by the day's events that I didn't even feel like painting, let alone doing homework, when I trudged to my room. I figured that everything that was due the next day I had already done, and all of my other homework could wait until tomorrow. My entire body felt tired from the emotional ups and downs of the day, and I began to wonder if maybe there was some sort of bug going around, and if Karen had given it to me. I concentrated all my efforts on going to sleep, and after what seemed like hours, sleep finally overtook me, giving me a dreamless eight hours before my alarm went off.

My wardrobe wasn't difficult to pick out that day, since Karen wasn't exactly the complicated type. I wore khaki pants with white sandals and a white form-fitting T-shirt. With my hair pulled back into a short ponytail, I slung my white backpack over my shoulder and made my way out the door. I noticed my mom's car in the driveway, which meant she'd had a long night and must have been sleeping. When she didn't bother opening the garage to pull her car in, I knew she'd gotten home much later than she'd want to let on.

I got into my own silver car and drove to school in silence. I had called David the night before to tell him not to talk to me today so that if Nate happened to walk by, he wouldn't see me kissing some boy, and then trying to flirt with him. It had to seem like I was available, or this would never work. David hadn't been happy with this idea, and I couldn't blame him. Even I wasn't happy with this, and I was the one making the rules.

Pulling into the busy school parking lot, I glanced down at the clock on my dashboard. I only had about five minutes before the bell rang, so I'd have to seek Nate out quickly. I made my way to the cafeteria and pulled an apple from my backpack. This, of course, was simply a prop to make it look like I had a legitimate excuse to be in the cafeteria. I spotted Nate easily enough. His light brown hair and rosy cheeks gave him away pretty quickly. His back was to me, and his shoulders were hunched over as if he, too, were exhausted. *There's definitely a bug going around*, I thought glumly.

Pulling on the hair in my ponytail to make sure it was firmly in place, I slid onto the bench next to Nate, causing him to jump slightly. When he looked up at me, I realized that he looked almost as pale as Karen had the day before. His cheeks were still bright red, but I suspected he could be frozen to death and his cheeks would remain naturally rosy. I wondered for a moment if perhaps Nate had gotten Karen sick, but thoughts like that didn't get my job done, so I pushed them away to concentrate on what I was doing now.

"Are you Nate?" I asked sweetly, letting an innocent smile play on my lips. He paid absolutely no attention to my full lips as some boys did when I talked to them, and I was instantly reminded that this was going to be a difficult job.

"Yeah, I am . . . why?" It didn't seem to be enough of a happy occurrence that a pretty girl was sitting with him; he was apparently the questioning type and needed a reason for this phenomenon.

"I'm a friend of Karen's," I said, my voice still oozing with honey. This got a reaction out of him, and he instantly straightened up and scooted closer to me, looking into my eyes intently.

"Is she all right?" he asked quickly, an urgency in his voice that I found touching. I was a bit puzzled by this reaction but responded to it with perfect cordiality.

"Oh, yes, she's fine. She's just feeling a bit under the weather." I gave him a winning smile that was a mixture of sympathy for my supposed best friend and allure for him. He didn't react to it in the slightest.

"Oh, good," he breathed, obvious relief lining his voice.

"I, on the other hand," I said as I scooted closer to him, "am all alone today. I was supposed to sit with Karen since it's my first day at school and everything, but she's sick, so I don't know a single person here." I batted my eyelashes at him a bit, and he cleared his throat and scooted away. At least I was making him nervous, that much was evident.

"Well, I'll be here at break and lunch if you need someone

to sit with, but if you'll excuse me, I need to go to my first class. Can you find yours all right?" All of this was said with such a polite concern that I couldn't lie to the boy, so I simply nodded my head and watched him walk away. I checked my watch once more and saw that there were only two minutes until the bell rang. Letting out a deep sigh, I threw the apple back into my backpack and stood up, only to have hands circle my waist from behind to rest lightly on my stomach. I turned my head with a shocked look of confusion to find David resting his chin on my shoulder.

"That didn't seem to go well," he remarked without any malice. There was only mild interest in his voice. He may not like my line of work, but at least he liked me enough to know when he shouldn't tease me too much.

"Not at all," I answered as I tilted my head to the side so that our cheeks were touching. I knew I shouldn't be so close to David when I was in character to break someone up, but I knew Nate would be halfway to his first class right now anyway, so I didn't see much point in enforcing that rule.

"Well," David began, gearing up for what sounded like the beginnings of a pep talk, "after what you told me yesterday, I think your best bet for this one might just be to tell him the truth. I mean, you may be the most beautiful girl ever, but that boy's got it bad. He's not going to take any bait you put out there." This all made sense, but the one thing David didn't understand was that I couldn't tell him the truth because Karen had told me not to.

"What if I'm not allowed to?" I asked, wondering what he might have to say to that little detail.

"I think Karen should be grateful to you for getting the job done, so I don't think she should be able to put too many stipulations on exactly *how* it's done. This really is probably the only way to complete this assignment so I can finally have you all to myself." He kissed my cheek lightly after saying this, pulling me closer to him. I placed my hands on top of his where they rested on my stomach and I closed my eyes. I felt so comfortable and safe with him there. It was such a weird feeling to have after only knowing him for a short time. I hoped beyond everything that jumping into this relationship so fast wouldn't come back to bite me in the butt later.

"I guess that's my only option," I agreed quietly.

When the bell rang, David and I went our separate ways, fully aware that we wouldn't be able to see each other for the rest of the day. After psychology I sought Nate out and found him just where he had said he'd be. I was afraid that after our interaction that morning, he would have found somewhere to hide from me until Karen came back to school the next day, so I was slightly shocked to see he'd kept his word. Then again, Nate just seemed to be that kind of guy—the kind who kept his word.

I slid into the spot next to him, yet again, and startled him, yet again. He looked up at me with what I thought looked like exasperation. "Hi," he said, his eyes returning to the book in front of him. I looked down at the title written across the top of each page and almost laughed when I read *Romeo and Juliet*. I had to quickly compose myself and put on a neutral face.

"English class," he said, following my gaze to the source of my amusement. Those two words were all I needed to jump right in to my job.

"So I've been hanging out with Karen for a while now," I started, gauging his reaction, which was absolutely unreadable. He didn't even look up from his book to talk to me, so I pushed on. "She's so much fun to hang out with." I looked at him once more and got nothing. It was like talking to a brick wall. If I hadn't seen him act so lively with Karen only the day before, I would have wondered what she saw in this guy. If he were like this with her, it would be like having a relationship with a teapot or a loaf of bread.

The only way to get this job done, apparently, would be to just drop my normal lines without waiting for his reactions and just see where to go from there. "So since we've been hanging out so much she's really started thinking about how much she likes to just be one of the girls." Still absolutely no reaction from Nate. "She's kind of realized that she'd like some freedom in her life . . . you know . . . not being tied down and all?" I wasn't really doing a good job at cushioning the blow, but it wasn't my fault. This guy was so head over heels for Karen that he wouldn't respond if a supermodel came and flirted with him. Not that I was comparing myself to a supermodel.

"So, I'm really sorry . . . I guess this is my fault for giving her a taste of single life, but she wants to break up with you," I finally said, his lack of reaction making me bold enough to just come right out and say it. I suppose I thought maybe he wouldn't react to that either and I'd have completed my job with no verbal backlash from the dumpee. I was wrong, of course, but not in the way I expected to be wrong.

"She doesn't want to break up with me," he said simply, his eyes still trained on the page in front of him. I wondered if he was actually reading the play or just keeping it there so that he wouldn't have to look at me.

"Yes, she does," I said, almost defensively, as if he were calling me a liar by not believing me.

"No, she doesn't," he countered. His voice was still neutral, like he was telling me that the capital of California was Sacramento. Finally, after a long silence of my confusion and his stubborn insistence, he looked up from the book.

"Who are you really?" he asked, with a resigned curiosity.

"I told you, I'm Karen's friend," I repeated. He shook his head at this but kept his eyes trained on mine.

"I've known Karen her whole life. We've been friends since we could talk. She only has a small handful of friends and most of them are homeschooled." My mouth hung open slightly from his completely out of the blue response. I hadn't expected him to know her so well, but then again, I had to remind myself that I wasn't dealing with a normal high school relationship. "So who are you?" he asked again.

"Amelia," I answered, though that didn't really answer his question.

"And she sent you to try to break up with me because she didn't want to do it herself?" he asked. This boy really was more astute than I gave him credit for. I nodded dumbly, wondering what I was supposed to do now. I felt like a spy whose identity had just been compromised, except I didn't exactly have the option of setting off a smoke bomb to make my great escape.

Nate closed the book that lay on the table in front of him. "Listen, Amelia. I know you think you're helping her out, but you're really not. Karen's mom is just overprotective of her because of her condition." He looked at me, searching my face for some scrap of understanding to see how much I actually knew about Karen.

"Condition?" I repeated with my brows drawn together in confusion.

"When she was little she got scarlet fever and it left her with a weak immune system. Now the smallest bug going around makes her sick. It was a battle just for her mom to let her go to a public school, so a boyfriend has always been completely out of the question." He kept his eyes trained on mine as though he were willing himself to be strong and continue on with the story of a life I was oblivious to. "As you can imagine, her mom is a little wary of Karen kissing boys or holding hands when she needs to be kept away from any germs. We've always been really careful, though. If I get even the smallest cold, I won't even come to school since we have a lot of the same classes. I wash my hands every five seconds when I'm around her, and we only kiss if we're both completely healthy."

His words were so heartfelt and concerned that I couldn't believe I'd actually set out to break them up. The fact that Nate was willing to risk a normal life just to be around Karen was almost too much for me to comprehend.

"She thinks she needs to break up with me because of her mom, but I know that if her mom knew how careful we were, she wouldn't object to our relationship. Karen's being unreasonable, though. She's terrified that if I ask, her mom will take her out of public school and she'll never see me." Now Nate looked down, the weight of the situation clearly on his shoulders. "I don't know what to do," he concluded quietly. I bit my lip and looked down also. What could he do? I didn't know Karen well, but maybe since she'd trusted me with the disposal of a relationship she was so fully invested in, she would trust my advice to let Nate talk with her mother.

"Maybe I can try talking to her. Karen, I mean. Maybe if I could get her to see reason, she'd let you talk to her mother. That way her mom would know there were ground rules to govern your relationship, since Karen is so fragile." I looked at him hopefully, finding that I actually wanted to save this relationship, even though my job had always been to destroy them. Maybe it was my connection with David that had sparked it, but I had a lot of hope for Karen and Nate.

"That might work," he said as he lifted his head to look at me. His eyes held a small spark of hope that I couldn't ignore.

"I'll call her later and see if you can come meet her mom tomorrow after school when she picks Karen up." At these words Nate looked a bit doubtful.

"*If* she's in school tomorrow. When she gets sick, Karen usually stays out of school for at least a week."

"Well, then, you'll just have to meet her mom on your own terms away from school. Besides, it'll look like you're much more serious about this if you go out of your way to meet her mom." I'd had some experience in the relationship world, and though my expertise didn't involve much hands-on practice, I knew what impressed people and how to really show them that you meant business.

"All right, it's a deal," Nate said, the spark of life that I'd seen in him the day before lighting once more. "Thanks, Amelia," he said as the bell rang and he made his way to class. I had to admit that I felt pretty good about myself as I walked to my English class. Of course, there was the question of exactly how I'd get Karen to accept my terms, but that was just a small detail.

I didn't have any time to work out my plan of attack during English because our teacher had decided that we needed to write a timed essay. She gave us a topic and started the timer, and I quickly learned that no one should ever write for two hours straight. By the time I left English for lunch, my hand was cramping and covered in ink.

I walked quickly to my spot by the library after stopping off to tell Nate that I'd be calling Karen in a few short minutes. David was there in my usual spot with a laptop in front of him, typing away furiously. I cleared my throat to try to break the intense look of concentration on his features. His face instantly brightened when he saw me, and he quickly put the laptop away.

"Homework," he said simply with a nod toward his

backpack, where the computer now resided.

I sat down and told him everything that had happened during break and what my current plan was as I pulled out my cell phone, which was pale blue today.

"Wow," he said simply, as I grabbed Nate's fact sheet to retrieve Karen's number. "Is your work always this crazy?" he asked me, though after watching me for a year I was sure he knew.

"Never," I answered. "It's weird for me to stumble across people who actually care for each other, let alone people who care for each other but can't be together because of things that are, for the most part, out of their control. I just really want to help them." David smiled at me warmly.

"And that's why I like you so much. You're a good person." I smiled back at him but looked down at the phone, not used to receiving genuine compliments that didn't revolve around my good looks. "Even if your typical day involves destroying innocent boy's lives," he added with a grin.

"I knew it was coming," I said with a shake of my head and a smirk.

Punching in the number Karen had given me, I rehearsed what I would say to her one more time.

"Hello?" came a familiar but weak voice on the other end.

"Karen?" I asked, even though I knew it was her.

"Hi, Amelia," she said quietly. I was surprised that she recognized my voice or possibly my number, but I continued on without any pause.

"How are you feeling? I heard you actually got sick." I knew I sounded guilty even though her real illness had nothing to do with me.

"I'm all right. It's just a small flu, but I should be fine in a few days." I heard a cough on the other end, and then she resumed her thoughts. "Did you talk to Nate yet?" I knew this was coming. In fact, it was the only reason I had called her, but I still felt unprepared to answer that question.

"So here's the thing, Karen. I talked to Nate but he wanted nothing to do with me because he's so in love with you." I paused for a moment but got only silence on the other end, so I took that as a sign to keep going. "So he ended up figuring out that you had sent me just to break up with him, and then he explained why you were doing it in the first place." Still silence. If I didn't know better, I would have thought that Nate and Karen had the most boring, silent relationship ever. "So anyway . . . I didn't break you guys up. I'll give you your money back and everything, but I have something I want to talk to you about."

"What is it?" she asked with a yawn.

"I want you to let Nate talk to your mom about you two."

"No," she said instantly, and with such authority I couldn't believe it had come from little, fragile Karen.

"What do you mean 'no'?" I asked.

"If he talks to my mom she'll know about us, and she'll take me away from the school and away from him," she whispered, and I suspected her mom was nearby.

"You don't know that," I responded, hoping I sounded more convincing than I felt.

"Yes, I do. She's so afraid I'll get sick just from being at school, she'd never let me near him." I thought this over for a moment, trying to find some sort of compromise.

"Well, maybe Nate could talk to her and you guys could set some rules. He already told me how careful you are. Surely that will show your mom how serious you both are about staying safe." I heard a choked sound on the other end of the line that sounded like a sob. "Or what if you went back to being homeschooled and Nate could still be your boyfriend? That way you'd be away from the threat of hundreds of kids and trade that in for just one boy." I thought it sounded like a reasonable proposal. After all, Nate had told me that Karen's friends were all homeschooled, and he was the only one she knew at the school anyway. If it meant getting to keep Nate in her life, I couldn't see why she wouldn't want to just stop going to a public school. It's not like she would miss the cafeteria food.

There was a long moment of silence in which I wondered if Karen had hung up or fallen asleep. After a minute or so of the silent hum of ambient noise, Karen's voice sounded on the other line. "It's worth a shot," she said finally, instantly bringing a smile to my face.

"Perfect," I said, a bit more enthusiastically than was necessary. David gave me an odd look, but I ignored it and continued. "I'll see if Nate can drop by your house tomorrow to talk to her. Don't worry, Karen. This is going to work. I just know it." We ended our conversation after a few more reassurances. I knew I shouldn't make promises to her if I couldn't definitely keep them, but I was just so sure that this whole plan would succeed that I couldn't see any other outcome.

"So everything's all right, I take it?" David asked beside me.

"I think it is. Nate's going to talk to Karen's mom tomorrow. He's going to ask if she can go back to being homeschooled in exchange for the freedom to date him. Personally I don't see how her mother can refuse. Trading in 3,000 kids for just one potential threat has to be a pretty appealing offer," I said confidently.

"Unless she feels that Nate poses a greater threat than those 3,000 kids," David replied with a sigh. "From what I've seen of her, Karen wouldn't be the type to go around kissing 3,000 students, just passing them in the hallways, not even making physical contact." As much as I hated how grim his outlook on my plan was, I couldn't deny that it was a legitimate argument, and one I'd have to be prepared for. "And there's always the possibility that she'll agree to the terms and then go back on the offer once she has her daughter out of school," he continued, quite unnecessarily.

"You certainly have a glum outlook on human nature," I said in annoyance.

"I was trying to catch a con artist for a year, so I had to start thinking of every possibility," he replied with a cheeky grin.

"I'm not a con artist," I corrected with indignation. "I'm a breakup artist."

sixteen

After school that day David was waiting for me by my car. I walked, a bit faster than normal, to meet him and instantly dropped my backpack on the ground once I was close enough to throw my arms around him. He laughed at my enthusiasm but I buried my face in the small space where his shoulder and neck came together. His wonderful smell was strongest there, and I considered never moving again. I kissed his neck softly, which made him shiver beneath me.

"Well, if I really am just a job, then you're pulling out all the stops," he said with a laugh. I leaned back slightly with my arms still around his neck so that I could get a better look at him. I had been thinking about David all through biology and had come to the conclusion that I didn't get to spend enough time with him today. Ever since we'd started officially dating, we hadn't really had time to ourselves to just be alone and talk. I didn't know nearly enough about him and everything he knew about me he had found out from a distance. That was no way to start a relationship.

"So I was thinking today," I began tentatively. His face became expectant, as if he thought I was going to break things off right then and there. I let that thought stew with him for a moment, just because I seemed to get some sort of sick pleasure out of the fact that he cared enough about me to worry. "I was thinking that you should come over today . . . Right now, actually." This obviously hadn't been what he was expecting, and his face brightened.

"To your house?" he asked, as a confirmation of what I had just said.

"Well, yeah. My mom is never home so you don't have to do the whole 'meeting the parents' thing just yet." I realized the second that I said my mom wouldn't be there that he could have easily taken a different motive from my asking him over to an empty house. "It'd just be nice to talk somewhere that isn't school," I added hastily.

"I'd like that," he said, after I spent what felt like an eternity of watching his face shift between some unheard thoughts. "Should I just follow you there?" he asked.

"Yeah, it's not too far from here," I answered happily. He dropped his hands from my waist and said, "I'll see you there."

It felt odd to have someone following me to my house. In my whole life I'd never had anyone over to my house to see me. Every birthday party had simply consisted of my mom and I going out to eat somewhere, and even those events had stopped with my thirteenth birthday. Now my birthdays consisted of my mother leaving me a twenty-dollar bill on the counter with a quickly scribbled note that read "Happy Birthday! Hope you have a great day! Love, Mom."

Even though it had only been a day since David and I had resolved our differences and decided to be an official couple, everything seemed so different. Life just held more possibilities now that I had allowed myself to experience it. Before David I hadn't really thought that I needed any changes in my life. Everything was just fine the way it was, with the occasional plague of loneliness that lasted a few days. Now that I had changed my views so completely, it felt as if I could breathe for the first time. It was like David had enabled me to fill a hole inside of me that I hadn't even known was there to begin with. It was a wonderful feeling, and I couldn't get enough of it.

We arrived at my house ten minutes later, me pulling into the driveway and David parking along the sidewalk. There was a nice looking black car near the sidewalk across the street, and I wondered for a moment if the neighbors were having the president over for dinner or something. These thoughts were quickly erased, however, when David emerged from his old blue car in all of his glory. I smiled at him and held out my hand, implying that he should take it. Luckily he was quick on the uptake and immediately obliged.

"You know, as we were coming here, I realized I've already been to your house. I didn't really need to follow you," he said matter-of-factly. I simply shrugged at this statement and turned the key in the lock on our front door. As we walked through the house to get to the living room, I decided to kick off the conversation. I vaguely registered that the house smelled a bit like smoke, but I didn't see a fire so I figured a window must have been opened to the smells outside.

"Since we're getting to know each other better, there's something I've been wondering," I said with a glance in his direction. "Are your parents married or divorced?" As the words were coming out of my mouth we turned into the living room where my mother stood with a man in a business suit. David and I stopped dead in our tracks, and I automatically dropped his hand, though I wasn't sure why. It wasn't like holding hands was a crime. My mother looked equally as shocked and I noted with profound embarrassment that her hair was disheveled with a button undone on the middle of her white blouse. It looked as if she had been pretty hastily put together. The man was in better shape, though his graying hair was sticking up a bit in the back.

I could feel my face turning red at the sight before me and I tried not to think of what the whole scene would look like to an outsider. Like mother, like daughter—I'm assuming is what that outsider would think. I kept my emotions under control, reminding myself that David and I were just going to talk and get to know each other, so I had absolutely nothing to feel guilty about. My mother, on the other hand . . .

"Amelia, what are you doing home?" she said, in what I'm sure she was hoping was an offhand, disinterested way.

"School always gets out at this time," I said simply, looking anywhere but at the man standing beside my mother.

"Of course it does, dear," she said, trying to salvage the "unfit mother" image she had just pinned on herself with her question. "Amelia," she said, pulling herself back together. "This is Lawrence Everett." She motioned to the man next to her, who gave me a winning smile and held out his hand. I reluctantly shook it and got a nose full of the cigarette smell I'd noticed earlier.

Lawrence Everett wore an expensive suit. His graying hair was slicked back in a businesslike manner that made him look like a snake. I also noted that he had a gold band on his left hand ring finger.

The situation was bad, but it wasn't one of those bad situations that has a sort of bad thing that can be overlooked. It was full of bad. There was the fact that, no matter how much David had figured out about me after watching for a year, he didn't know that my mother's relationship with me was non-existent. And there was always the little concern of the ring on Mr. Snake's finger. I looked at the ground now, though I knew it was my turn to introduce my company. I didn't know if I should spring the title of "boyfriend" on my mom as a small, shocking payback, or just say "friend" so that we could avoid any further conversation. The room was silently expectant, waiting for me to fill the void.

"I'm David," my wonderfully observant boyfriend said by my side. I was so relieved that he sensed my lack of ability to speak that I could have kissed him for it, though I would obviously refrain just at the moment. "Amelia and I are in the same English class and I haven't been doing so well on my tests, so the teacher suggested I get some help from her best student." His story was so convincingly told that I even believed it for a second.

"I'm not the best student," I said, in what I hoped sounded like embarrassed modesty. The statement at least gave me a reason to keep my eyes on the ground so that no one would be able to tell how red my face was getting or how watery my eyes were becoming.

"Well, that's nice of you, young lady," Mr. Snake said. I simply nodded.

"I was just showing Lawren—Mr. Everett some houses and I forgot a key here, so we came to retrieve it. We have a lot of places to look at before the day is through, though, so I'll see you later tonight Amelia. Nice to meet you David," my mother said in one breath. She swept Lawrence out of the room quickly, and I didn't move until I heard the door shut and his expensive car roar to life across the street. Oh yeah, that outsider would definitely think, "like mother, like daughter."

As the silence in the room slowly grew deafening, I tried to blink back the tears that were threatening to pour down my cheeks. It was one thing to not be involved in your own mother's life, but it was a completely different thing to find that what little involvement you have is discovering her heinous secrets. My bottom lip shook with the effort of holding back any emotion, and I couldn't bear to look at David. I couldn't even begin to imagine what he must think of me: "No wonder she does what she does—look at how messed up her home life is." To my surprise, however, he didn't say anything. He didn't try to skew the truth so that it looked better than it was. He didn't try to say it was no big deal. He didn't lie to me. He just wrapped his arms around me and held me to his chest while I began to sob, and that alone told me more about him than any POIs could have.

My mother didn't come home that night, which didn't really surprise me, but David didn't seem to be scared off by the fact that it was a possibility that she could just wander in with some man. Instead of fleeing the scene when it was polite to do so, he told me I should go upstairs and get my homework done, and he would make dinner for me. I protested this idea many times, telling him that I was fine and didn't need to be taken care of, but he won in the end.

We did compromise a bit, however, and I ended up doing my homework at the kitchen table while he looked through cupboards until he found what he needed for whatever dish he was planning on making. I tried to make pleasant small talk at first, offering smiles that were far from genuine when I really just felt like crying some more, but eventually David stopped that by simply saying, "You don't have to pretend to be happy just because I'm here. You don't even need to fill in the empty space with words if you don't want to. If you feel like breaking a dish, by all means, go right ahead . . . I'll even join you."

His smile and complete understanding of exactly how I felt at that moment caught me off guard. I couldn't understand how I could know someone for such a short amount of time and still be so completely in tune with him. "Thank you," I said with a small, sad smile. I wasn't feeling happy by any stretch of the imagination, but David's mere presence kept me from feeling completely lost. I figured that once he left and I was really all alone, I'd have some sort of breakdown and that was something I definitely wasn't looking forward to.

Miraculously enough, I finished all of my homework in an hour. I didn't think I'd be able to concentrate with so much on my mind, but David's insistence that we didn't have to talk if I didn't want to, and the continual sounds of him cooking kept me on track. By the time I packed up my completed homework, David had cooked some sort of baked chicken and mashed potatoes dish. He brought the plate to me along with a glass of juice and sat down opposite me at the table.

"I didn't know you could cook," I said hoarsely. My voice seemed to be rebelling from the hour of crying and the hour of not speaking.

"Well, I guess there's the first answer to our twenty questions then," he said with a warm smile. "Do you want to keep going or should we take turns?"

"Your turn," I answered simply.

"All right." He stopped for a moment, taking a sip of juice while thinking of what to ask. I figured he was trying to think of something he could ask me without bringing up the events of earlier today. "What do you want to study at college?"

"Marriage counseling," I said with a small laugh. The poor boy had tried so hard to avoid bringing up any unpleasant memories, and here he had asked the question that would lead right into that horrible discussion.

"Oh," he said awkwardly, which made me actually smile. I figured I'd relieve the situation instantly and ask him the question I'd asked before.

"So are your parents divorced or still together?"

"Still together. Have been for years," he said vaguely. I raised an eyebrow at this. It was sad, but I was always more shocked to find out that a couple was still together than I was to find out that they were divorced.

"When did your parents get divorced?" he asked me. I guess since I had opened that up as an acceptable topic I should have expected that question.

"I don't know that they ever really did," I said honestly. "My father just kind of left when I was six. I don't know if they ever made it official. My mom hasn't said a word about him since that day, and I haven't had any desire to bring it up with her . . . especially now," I mumbled. David gave my foot a little nudge under the table, and I quickly went on with the questioning. "So what do your parents do?"

"Well, my mom works from home. She makes jewelry and sells it online. And my dad is a science professor over at the university in Camarillo." I smiled at him. I could just imagine David having dinner at home with his parents— having pleasant conversations about things that had nothing to do with older married men. "You know the university where my dad works used to be a mental hospital. I guess that's fitting, since once we go to college we'll pretty much be losing our minds." This made me laugh. It was a real, genuine, happy laugh, and I loved David for bringing it out in me.

By the time we finished our dinner, it was starting to get late. I wondered when David would decide to go home. I didn't want to make him feel obligated to stay with his sad, emotionally damaged girlfriend, but I also didn't want him to leave, knowing that when he did I'd have too much time to think about the things I'd seen today and I might lose it.

I insisted on doing the dishes since he had made dinner, so he sat on the couch in our living room with his laptop in front of him. He was typing just as intensely as he had been at lunch when I finished the dishes. I could see a document open on his screen, filled with writing, but I didn't want him to catch me looking over his shoulder and think I was spying on him so I cleared my throat to make my presence known.

"Do you need to call your parents or anything?" I asked as I sat on the couch next to him. He closed his computer and slid it under the couch before handing me the remote to the TV. He knew me too well already. I really needed anything that could let me empty my brain of all significant thoughts, like watching TV for hours on end.

"I already did. I told them I'd be out late tonight and that I might stay at a friend's." He looked over at me questioningly, asking if it was all right in that one expression.

"Good," I said simply, happy that I wouldn't be left alone with myself. After a few episodes of old black and white TV shows, David apparently felt it was time to talk.

"So are you all right?" he asked, and I instantly knew what he was asking about.

"I don't know," I said. "I never wanted to know that my home life was so . . . just . . . messed up." I looked over at him and I could feel the burning in my eyes again. "Sometimes I go a week without even seeing my mom once." I sighed in resignation as a hot tear slid down my cheek.

"Amelia, it's not like I'm going to judge you because

of that. I just want to be able to make you happy." He put his arm around me, and I let my head rest on his shoulder. As I closed my eyes and took in his scent, I was overcome with just how exhausted I was. If I had any more emotionally stressful days, I'd have to start getting more sleep. My breathing slowed as a heavy lethargy rolled over me.

"Are you tired?" he asked, though his voice seemed distant.

"Mmhmm," I answered wordlessly. I could feel David moving beside me, but I wasn't quite sure what exactly he was doing. After a little jostling I knew that he was lying behind me with an arm draped over my shoulders. I took his hand and held it against me like a blanket. Then I let myself fall asleep in his arms.

seventeen

"Amelia?" I heard a soft, familiar voice whisper in my ear. I could feel a warm body beside me and the weight of an arm resting over me, which made me smile. David even smelled wonderful in the morning. I nestled my head against his chest and breathed him in, keeping my eyes closed in an attempt to fall back asleep. "Amelia?" came the voice again. "Amelia, we're late for school . . . really late for school." The words spoken by the voice vaguely registered with me, but I knew they were something I should be reacting to. As much as I tried to stir panic within me, I just couldn't seem to pull myself out of this comfortable place.

"How late?" I mumbled against David's neck.

"Let's just say that if we don't leave now, we'll be in danger of walking in late to our second class . . . first period's already over." Now I was awake, but still, there was just no room for panic right now. I'd spent a lot of last night crying, and the whole ordeal had just worn me out, so to wake up next to David was the best possible feeling in the world at the moment. I didn't want to wake up in an empty house with a note from my mother lying about where she was.

I yawned and pulled myself closer to him so that we

were completely entwined together. "I don't want to get up," I whined wearily, letting my foot rub against his. I could hear him laugh softly at this protest, and he began to move. I knew he was getting up, but I just didn't want to have any part of that. "If we walk in late to our second class we'll be drawing more attention to ourselves," I said reasonably. "We should go in during lunch when lots of other students will be leaving and returning to campus." I waited for his response, now finally opening my eyes.

David's shaggy blond hair was sticking up in various directions, and his cheeks looked a bit stubbly, but his green eyes were just as bright as ever. I didn't even want to think about what I looked like. He looked thoughtful for a moment and then said, "I guess that makes sense." I had won. It was a nice feeling, and I celebrated the victory by giving him a small kiss. It felt somewhat scandalous that I had woken up in the arms of this boy and was now kissing him while lying on the couch, but I knew it was innocent, so it didn't bother me. He smiled at me and pulled me against him so I could rest my head on one of the throw pillows on the couch. Our faces were just inches away, and he rested his forehead against mine.

"Are you hungry?" he asked after a moment of silence.

"I'm more tired than anything," I admitted. We must have gotten a good ten hours of sleep, but I felt more exhausted than when I'd fallen asleep the night before.

"Well, then why don't you get some more sleep and I'll make some eggs . . . do you like eggs?" I nodded happily and closed my eyes once more. He gave me the smallest of kisses and stood from the couch, allowing me to spread out. We didn't have a particularly large couch, and it felt good to be able to stretch my arms and legs. I could only imagine how poor David had to feel. I'd slept on his arm all night, which couldn't have been too amazingly comfortable for him.

I fell in and out of a light sleep and was eventually awakened by a wonderful smell. When he'd said he was going to make eggs, that must have been a code word for eggs, bacon, and toast, because there was a lot more going on in the kitchen than just eggs. I stood up groggily and made my way to the bathroom to do some damage control before going back into the kitchen. Looking in the mirror I was met with a frightening sight. My hair was everywhere, my face had little red splotches from being warmly nestled against David, and my eyeliner made me look like a raccoon. Sleeping in my clothes had been uncomfortable enough, but the collar of my shirt had left deep red lines all over my neck, no doubt from my constant wriggling during the night. I quickly brushed my teeth and washed my face, which at least got rid of the red splotches and makeup. Then I ran a brush through my untamed hair and pulled it back into a short ponytail.

Feeling that this was as good as I would be able to look on such short notice, I made my way into the kitchen where David already had two plates of food set up for us, complete with glasses of orange juice. I wasn't quite sure where he had found all of these ingredients, but then again my mother and I never cooked. We lived on take-out food and leftovers. Who knew that so much could be made with whatever we had stored in our cupboards?

I breathed in the aroma of the freshly made food and gave David a satisfied smile. "I still can't believe you can cook so well," I said as we began to eat.

"I can't really do much. Just basic stuff," he answered modestly.

"My cooking skills extend to reheating . . . and that's all.

So that makes this pretty impressive." He looked down at his food, but I saw a pleased smile on his face, which I pretended not to notice.

We talked about our upcoming date on Friday and conveniently stepped around any conversation having to do with the events of the previous day. When we had finished breakfast I told David I'd get the dishes so that he could run home to change his clothes and meet me at school. We had a brief farewell on the doorstep, and I went back into the house to take care of the breakfast dishes. I couldn't believe how everything had turned out all right after what I'd seen yesterday. I still wasn't ready to really mentally examine the ordeal, but I felt that I had a secure enough grasp of the situation that I wouldn't break down anymore.

David had been such a help both intentionally and unintentionally that I couldn't seem to comprehend just how much he was beginning to mean to me. I tried to ignore the little nagging possibilities that this couldn't last forever and that we would someday join the ranks of failed high school relationships, but it made me wonder if that was how everyone felt. Surely David and I had a special relationship, far above the ones I had helped to destroy. But what if that wasn't the case? What if all relationships started out with that same exciting hope that maybe you've actually found something special? Did that make me a bad person for destroying what little spark of hope these people had? Was I just an embodiment of social failure because I wasn't able to interact normally with other people? And had I made it my life's work to bring them down with me?

That had certainly never been my intention, but what if through all of my self-assurance that I was helping people, I'd actually become something bad? These thoughts were exactly the reason I needed David around. I didn't think so much about these kinds of things when he was with me. But then again, did that mean I was simply using him as a convenience? Did I want him because he fixed something in me? Wasn't that what made people love each other? They found their missing piece, the person who completed them, and they wanted to stay with that person so they could continue to feel whole?

The deep thoughts were beginning to wear me out, so I quickly finished the dishes, trying to keep away thoughts about the meaning of life or the secret to immortality. Then I made my way to my bedroom to change. I looked through my closet to pick out what I'd wear to school that day and realized I didn't have a job and could wear whatever I wanted. In fact, I could wear whatever I wanted for the rest of my life. I would actually have to develop a sense of style, which was a daunting task. After sixteen years of having no personality to speak of, I suddenly had to develop an entire persona. This was going to be difficult.

I looked through my many different styles of clothing and tried to find one that jumped out at me as being appealing. Nothing really seemed to grab my attention, sadly, and so in the end I wound up with blue jeans and a black tank top with my black and white canvas shoes. It was a boring selection, but it was all I could think of to wear. I tried to place this clothing choice into a category, but I couldn't seem to pin it down. It was kind of a mixture between punk, artsy, and classical. Then again, I guess I didn't need to attribute a label to myself to feel secure. I could just be Amelia and live with that.

I got to school about halfway through the lunch period, which was perfect, because some students would be streaming back in from the pizza place across the street by now. I made my way past the large statue of a knight in the main quad and over to the library where David was sitting, wearing blue jeans and a light blue, slightly distressed T-shirt. He grinned at me as I approached and, despite my best efforts to keep a straight face, I smiled back at him.

"Long time no see," he said as I sat down next to him. "I wasn't sure if you were hungry, but I didn't really get anything for lunch since we just ate . . . did you want something?" I found it endearing that he thought of every little way to make me comfortable.

"I'm fine," I said.

"So is this what you wear when you're being yourself?" he asked, looking me over with approval.

"I'm not sure. It's going to be an adjustment having to dress myself based on how I actually feel that day. I swear, it took me an hour to settle on jeans and a tank top." I shook my head at the absurdity that something so normal and effortless seemed to be so difficult for me.

"Well, I think it looks great, but I was wondering, now that you don't have to continually dye your hair anymore, what color do you think you'll settle—oh . . . Nate's coming over here," David said, cutting himself off mid-sentence. I looked over toward the quad to see Nate striding over. I couldn't read by his expression if he had already talked to Karen's mom or not. To be completely honest, I had completely forgotten about the whole situation until that very moment. When he was within earshot, I tried to put on an encouraging smile, hoping he was coming to deliver good news.

"Hey Nate, what's up?" I asked. A small smile was resting on his lips so I figured the news couldn't be all bad.

"I talked to Karen's mom last night. I know I was supposed to wait until today but I couldn't. I just wanted to sort things out already and . . . well, I couldn't help myself."

This report was nice to hear, but completely pointless until he actually told us how it went. Not wanting to deter him from his train of thought, though, I simply nodded encouragingly, willing him to continue. "She was really mad at first. I thought I'd completely messed things up, but after Karen calmed her down, we explained everything. We told her about all of the precautions we'd taken, about how Karen wouldn't mind going back to being homeschooled if it meant we'd be able to stay together." He stopped there, which was amazingly frustrating.

"And?" David and I asked in unison.

"And she said that as long as Karen agrees to be homeschooled and we run all dates by her first, she thinks it could be all right." Nate seemed ecstatic with this news. It had apparently been quite an effort for him to keep the smile from his face while telling us the story so that he didn't spoil the ending.

"That's wonderful, Nate," I said enthusiastically. The situation may still be a bit overbearing for my taste, but at least they were happy.

"I know!" he agreed wholeheartedly. "Thanks so much for helping," he added sincerely. "I'll have to remember to repay you someday," he said as he turned to leave.

"Wait!" I said suddenly, remembering that I hadn't actually broken them up. I fished my wallet out of my backpack and pulled out the fifty dollars Karen had given me. "Can you give this back to Karen?" I asked, holding the money out to Nate's retreating form.

"I'll repay the fifty dollars myself, and you keep that as a thank you from me. Besides, what you did for us is worth more money than that," he conceded happily. And with that, he was gone, walking with a bounce in his step back to the cafeteria.

"Well, I'd say that was a nice way to end your career," David said, looking at me.

"It is, isn't it?" I hadn't quite expected the end of my career to be such an easy transition. I'd always expected that I would miss something once it was over, that I'd feel empty or sad that the one constant in my life was no more. None of these feelings came, though. I felt completely at terms with my life and the changes it had taken for the better. I had David, I actually might have made friends with Nate and Karen, and everything was just fine. There was the problem of my mother and how she chose to spend her free time, but I suspected that I'd just have to accept that my mother and I would never understand each other. It was a sad reality, but it was one I could learn to live with.

David kissed me good-bye as the bell rang, and then I made my way to math. With only one class today, I actually felt like I might be able to handle the workload. Everything felt completely perfect. Too perfect. This should have been my first warning signal, but because I'd never experienced true happiness, I wasn't anticipating a change of course. Real life throws you curve balls, and mine was coming fast. I was about to discover that in "normal" life, just when things start to look up and you become comfortable, things fall apart when you least expect it. Of course, being the social virgin that I was, I blissfully went about, enjoying my comfort zone, not knowing that the "falling apart" phase was lurking just around the corner.

eighteen

I approached my locker after school, ready to deposit my math book and spend a lovely afternoon with David when I noticed a girl standing there. She wore stylish clothes that just reeked of designer labels. I suspected that she hadn't spent less than $100 on jeans in her life. Her hair was dyed blonde in the way that actually made you wonder if it was dyed or natural. That color had definitely come from a salon and not from a bottle.

I approached the girl warily, sure she was there to give me a job, or maybe tell me that I'd been switched at birth and her incredibly rich parents had decided to take me back under their wing as their own, pay for my college, buy me a new car, and generally make my life easy. That wasn't the case.

"Amelia Bedford?" she asked in a way that made her sound like a CSI agent trying to approach a murderer for questioning without scaring them off.

"Yes," I answered apprehensively.

"I'm Rachel McKlintock," she said, as if that name should mean a lot to me. It did ring a bell, of course. Everyone in school knew Rachel McKlintock's parents were something like the fourth wealthiest people in the state. This was quite a feat in California, if you take into account that it's where all the movie stars live. No one really knew why the McKlintocks had so much money, but that didn't really matter. If you're rich, you're rich.

"Okay," I said, still wondering why someone like Rachel McKlintock was approaching me.

"I have a job for you. I need to—"

"Oh no . . . sorry, I don't do that anymore," I said definitely. I didn't even want to let her get any further than that into her speech, or I just might not be able to say no.

"Since when?" she asked, the perfect picture of indignity. After all, she was Rachel McKlintock. Shouldn't everyone fall at her feet, ready to serve her?

"Since two hours ago," I said, waving her aside so I could get into my locker. She didn't budge . . . not that I had really expected her to.

"Well, what if I told you I was willing to pay a bit more than you normally charge?" she said. I knew she was going to say that, which was exactly why I didn't want her to go on talking. I groaned and looked around to make sure David wasn't there to witness this moment of weakness. It wasn't that I was actually considering listening to her proposal, but if she was going to throw it at me, I didn't have much of a choice. I could just refuse anyway.

"I'll give you five hundred dollars," she said, waiting for my reaction to this. My reaction was just what she likely had expected it to be. My eyes grew wide, and I stared at her in disbelief. "Here's the thing," she went on, not waiting for me to speak, "I've been dating this boy Alex because he's rich." Well, that was extreme honesty—at least she was able to admit it. "I guess he's cute and everything, but I'm just not that into him anymore. But my mom is so obsessed with me marrying him because if our families were joined by marriage it'll make her look good at the country club or something bogus like that." I suddenly felt like I was back in the Victorian period where someone was promised to someone else because his or her parents thought it was a good idea. I didn't have any pity for Rachel, though. Somehow she just wasn't exactly a pitiable person.

"So break up with him," I said, pointing out the obvious, for which I was sure she'd have a great excuse as to why this was impossible.

"My mom won't let me. I've told her a million times that I don't like Alex anymore, but she just doesn't get it. Unless he leaves me for someone, there's just no way I can get out of this. Even Daddy won't listen to me." She pouted slightly at this. Oh poor girl, even daddy wouldn't listen. How horrible her life must be.

"I'm really sorry about your . . . uh . . . situation, but I just can't help you. I'm quitting the business. Sorry." I tried once again to get into my locker, and she blocked me once more. This ritual was truly becoming old, and I crossed my arms in front of my chest and raised my eyebrows at the girl before me, almost asking for a reason to forcibly remove her from my locker.

"You seriously won't just take this one job for five hundred dollars?" she asked me, wondering why I was being so unreasonable in the face of so much money. Honestly, I was wondering that exact same thing, but I couldn't take the job after I swore to David that I wouldn't. That would make me just like all of the other girls I'd helped in the past. It would make my word cheap and our relationship and the trust it was built off of even cheaper.

"I seriously won't," I responded, matching her whiny yet authoritative tone. I turned to walk away, figuring I could live with keeping my math book in my backpack until tomorrow, when the girl grabbed me by the arm. I hate when people do that. It made me feel like a child being scolded. "What?" I shouted at her, causing her to jump a bit and heads to turn for just a second.

"One thousand," she said simply, and I wondered if I was hearing her correctly. I could have sworn she had just offered to give me one thousand dollars to break up with her boyfriend. It was a job that would probably take a day. I looked around me once more to see if David was nearby. Knowing him, he would be waiting by my car just so he could spend a few extra minutes with me. David. My wonderful, trusting boyfriend who helped me out when I needed him most. The one who wouldn't think I'd go back on my word because I'd promised him I'd stop my business. He was nowhere to be found, and I was pretty sure I was just about to sell my soul to the devil. And the devil was tapping her very expensive shoe on the concrete floor impatiently.

I pulled a blank fact sheet out of my backpack, having never gotten around to throwing them all away, and handed it to her. "Email me with this information and your phone number and don't come to school tomorrow. Fake sick," I said, feeling pretty scummy. I didn't think even David could argue with doing just one more job when it was paying so well. But did that mean I should tell him and risk having to give the job up?

"I'll bring you the money on Monday," she said matter-of-factly, as if $1,000 was like pocket change. I nodded wordlessly and watched her walk to the school parking lot. I knew I was lower than scum, but I just couldn't seem to think clearly. In the face of such an offer what else was I supposed to do? But should I expect David to understand that, or should I just keep it to myself on the off chance that he'd react badly?

I walked to my car dismally and sure enough David was waiting there, his face lighting up as he saw me approaching.

"What took you so long?" he asked, pulling me against him. He kissed my neck, making me feel worse and worse about my decision with every wonderful thing he said or did. "Do you want to come over to my house today? I kind of want you to meet my parents." On any other day that should have made me feel magnificent, but as it was I just felt like it was a knife in my heart.

"Actually, I'm not feeling too well . . . and I've got a lot of math homework, so I think I'm just going to go home and work on that," I said monotonously. David looked at me with concern and I knew what he was about to ask. "I'm fine. I'm just a little worn out. I think I'll probably finish up my math and just go to bed early." He kept his eyes trained on mine, the worry still evident. "Really. I'm fine. I'll see you tomorrow, all right?" He nodded and gave me a quick kiss before walking to his car, and I made my way home feeling pretty bad about myself.

I woke up the next morning with blonde hair and a relatively good idea of how I was going to get rid of Alex Swensen. The fact sheet Rachel had emailed the night before read:

Name—Alex Swensen
Age—18
POI—Parties, Travel, Tennis
Deadline—One week

Though this description of Alex was fairly predictable

and extremely stereotypical of what I'd always thought rich kids were like, it gave me something to go off of. For style I'd just copy Rachel and hope that Alex was relatively dim as far as conversation went. If he started talking about Italy or nineteenth-century European art, I was screwed. My wardrobe for the day consisted of a purple, sleeveless, high collared Victorian style top with ruffles down the front and a short black pleated skirt. I wore plain black flats on my feet and a sparkly purple rhinestone bracelet to tie the whole thing together. I pulled my bangs back on top of my head then pushed them forward with some bobby pins to give it that "rock star poof" (as I always called it) and curled the rest so that it fell in natural-looking ringlets around my face.

The effect was pretty flattering, but I wasn't sure what David would make of it. Through all of my plotting and planning the night before, I still hadn't come up with a way to keep David out of the picture. I thought that maybe if I could just stay away from our normal spot, he wouldn't even know I was at school. I had called him the night before and told him that I was starting to feel really sick and that I wouldn't be in school the next day. It was the exact same thing I was sure Rachel was doing at that moment. My only hope for pulling this off was that David wouldn't be looking for a blonde, and so hopefully he wouldn't be able to spot me. Another little detail that worked in my favor was the fact that Rachel and Alex apparently hung out by the tennis courts near the football field, far away from the library. I could use the south entrance instead of the east entrance so that I wouldn't run into David at all.

Though I felt like scum for deceiving him, I somehow figured that it was better that he never know rather than having him find out and get hurt. Obviously it would be better for me that way, but somehow it had to be better for him as well.

I drove to school, leaving myself just enough time to park in the side parking lot and barely make it to my class on time. I didn't want to run the risk of seeing David in the hallway on the way to class. I'd also have to remember to wait for a few minutes after the bell rang to make my way to the tennis courts, just in case he decided to loiter around the hallways today.

Miss Tess seemed to take note of my drastic change in style during psychology, but said nothing, as I knew she would. She had observed my happiness in the last few days and had made a few cryptic remarks about how love was in the air, but now she just stayed behind her desk and eyed me suspiciously from time to time. When the bell rang, I made a process of putting my things in my black leather purse and checking my appearance in a little hand mirror until Miss Tess actually had to kick me out of her class.

The tennis courts were nearby, and I wondered as I walked if Alex would have a group of friends with him or if he and Rachel hung out at the courts alone. If he was alone it would be much easier to get the job done, but I was used to having to work around friends, so either way I'd be fine. When I turned the corner to the brick wall separating the pool from the rest of the school I saw a blond boy walk by me. I thought for a split second that it was David and instantly lowered my gaze to the ground, though I knew I was just being paranoid.

Just as Rachel had promised, I found Alex at the tennis courts with a few male friends. I tried to ready myself for the upcoming job, but found that I had no desire for the tasks that I used to find at least mildly amusing. This really had become work for me. If I hadn't been lying to David about it, I was sure it would at least feel a bit more like it used to, but the new added layer of deception was taking its toll on my conscience. Still, I had gotten this far and it was too late to go back, so I made myself walk those few last steps to the group of boys. I put on an alluring smile for the tall, dark, and handsome boy in front of me.

Because I'd have to get Alex to break up with Rachel, I'd have to play this differently than all of my other conquests. I made no reference to Rachel as I shamelessly flirted with the boy before me. I simply told him that I had gotten lost looking for one of my classes because I was new and tragically not used to the discomforts of the public school system. This, of course, got him wondering about my background. I then hinted at my rich parents and good upbringing, all the while laying on the charm and completely ignoring his love-struck friends. This made him feel special, as I knew it would, but by the end of break he still hadn't made a move.

I was glad I wouldn't have to worry about the complexity of explaining to David that I had taken a job but I was slightly disappointed that Alex hadn't taken the bait enough to choose me over Rachel. I reasoned that, because it was a different type of job, it would take longer than my usual routine of breaking the news and cushioning the blow.

The routine at lunch followed much in the same pattern that the break time scene had. We flirted, he implied that he was single without coming right out and saying it, and I continued to get him interested in me. By the end of the day, I had still come up short, and I wondered if maybe Alex had to actually break up with Rachel before making a move on me because of his parents. It hadn't struck me before that these kids actually had an image to maintain. I guess I had just figured that because they were rich kids, they'd behave like spoiled celebrities who did stupid and scandalous things just to get noticed.

With this reassurance firmly in place, I walked to my car, thinking I'd give Alex the weekend to stew over my offer. I'd just get his number from Rachel and text him, hinting that I was really craving good company at a nice restaurant. It was my fatal flaw to assume everything would work itself out and so, I shouldn't have been at all surprised to see David leaning against my car, looking like he could murder someone.

I approached him cautiously, like a child who had dirtied their new and expensive Sunday clothes. He didn't say anything when I reached him, but he simply stared at me, a mixture of disbelief, anger, and hurt on his beautiful face. I didn't know what to say, though I knew I owed him some sort of explanation. My embarrassment flooded together with my stupid pride, telling me that I didn't have to explain myself to anyone. I looked down at the ground, refusing to speak first, and biting my lip to keep from telling him how sorry I was. How much I wanted to keep him in my life. How stupid it was of me to take on another job after promising I wouldn't. How much it hurt me that I'd lied to him. How I wanted him to forgive me and forget the whole thing.

Of course, I said none of that and just continued to stare at the ground. He looked for a moment as if he might say something, but then shut his mouth and walked away without a word, his face a mask of disappointment and sadness. The wetness on my cheeks served as a cruel reminder of my own stupidity. It seemed like I had been crying a lot that week.

nineteen

David didn't come to pick me up for our date that night, though I wasn't sure if I had really expected him to. What I did expect was an angry phone call or email. I expected an angry anything, really. Anything would have been better than the silence I experienced that Friday night. My mother was out, as usual, and I was beginning to wonder if she was just going to stay at some other house now that we'd had our little encounter. The house was completely empty and silent, just like my life. I had tried to call David several times, but he never picked up. I left at least four messages telling him I was sorry and that if he'd just let me talk to him I could explain everything, but it seemed like no matter what I did, he didn't feel compelled to call me back.

Saturday passed much in the same way. I saw my mother briefly in the kitchen as she was on her way out the door. She gave me a little nod of her head by way of a greeting but said nothing. I had finished my homework for the entire weekend the night before, which left me with absolutely nothing to do. I tried to paint, but found that I couldn't think of a single thing that would make me feel better.

After hours of sitting around staring at my paints, I picked up the phone and called Rachel.

"Hello?" said a groggy voice. It was almost one in the afternoon, so the fact that Rachel was still sleeping was quite a feat.

"Hey, it's Amelia," I said dully. "I was just wondering if Alex has broken up with you yet." Under any other circumstances that sentence would have sounded incredibly rude and out of place, but as it stood, it was really the only reason I could be calling Rachel.

"Not yet. He hasn't called me all weekend though, so I'm assuming that's a good sign. Maybe he's thinking it over and trying to find a way to let me down easy." She laughed at this, though I didn't see what was so amusing about it. "Anyways, if he doesn't call me on Sunday, I'll just ditch school Monday to give you another chance at getting him to do it. After that, I'm rescinding my offer."

"Don't worry, I'll take care of it," I said unenthusiastically.

"I figured you would," she said, and then the line went dead. I was beginning to notice that none of my clients seemed to posses the ability to say "good-bye" to end their phone conversations. They all just kind of hung up. Maybe it was because in their eyes I was more like the hired help—more like a vending machine than a human being. I ran my fingers through my blonde, messy hair, fully aware that I hadn't brushed it that morning, and searched through the contact list on my phone. I now had six numbers saved rather than just five, though it didn't make much of a difference, since that sixth number wouldn't answer my calls.

I hit send when the scroll illuminated David's name and got his voicemail once again.

"Hey, David, it's Amelia. I know you're probably sick of

all the messages I've left you, but I just want to talk. You can't really want to throw everything away without at least talking first, can you?" I paused for a second, though I knew the voicemail certainly wasn't going to answer me. "Anyway, I'm really sorry, and if you just let me explain, we might be able to work this out."

I paused again, feeling the urge to say something I knew was crazy after having only known this boy for such a short amount of time. Still, there it was, completely overpowering me and making me unable to think about anything other than David. It was that one emotion I thought didn't exist in the world. The one that I knew would probably scare him away if I uttered it when our relationship was in danger of falling apart. In the end, though, my feelings won out and I said the thing I knew I should just keep to myself. And that's how I ended my voicemail to him.

"I love you."

Saturday night came and went with absolutely no response from David, and I wallowed in my own self-pity. I knew I was being pathetic and love struck, but it felt like misery was just that much more intense after everything had been so perfect. I felt completely at a loss now that my other half was missing. I wouldn't have felt this if I hadn't known how wonderful it felt to be with someone you're so completely in tune with in the first place. The whole thing left me feeling empty, and I fell asleep that night crying.

Sunday morning passed without my notice. I didn't wake until two in the afternoon. Suddenly I felt like Rachel had the right idea, sleeping the day away. Nothing seemed so horrible if you just shut out the world for a while. I walked through the house to see if my mom was home, but found no one. I didn't even find a note saying she was out with a client. I guess she knew I'd just assume she was out with someone now, though "client" wasn't really the term I'd use.

I ate an apple and checked my phone for any new messages or missed calls but was met with nothing. I tried to ignore the sharp pain this left right above my stomach and decided to be semi-productive and take a long hot shower. I washed my hair thoroughly and scrubbed my skin until it felt raw, trying to wash away the creeping feeling that I had ruined something truly amazing. As I continued to endure the rest of this long day by myself, I spent time on all of the little extras. I needed anything to keep my mind occupied.

By the time I was done with my routine, I had perfectly curled hair, expertly applied makeup, and absolutely nowhere to go. I had, luckily, eaten up some time in the day, and I noticed that the sun was beginning to make its way toward the distant mountain range. I had gotten Rachel to give me Alex's number with the compromise that I'd go out on a date with him that Monday night, even though that was the furthest thing from what I wanted to be doing.

With nothing left for me to waste my time on, I went into the living room to watch some TV. There had to be something on that could distract me from my current state. As I went to sit on the couch, my foot hit something hard on the floor, causing me to yelp with pain. I looked down angrily to locate the source of my annoyance, only to see the corner of David's laptop sticking out from under the couch. *He must have left it when he made me dinner*, I thought excitedly. At least holding his laptop ransom could give me some excuse to see him again, even if it only meant seeing him for a second to give him the computer. At this point I was desperate. Any contact would make me feel better.

I quickly picked up my phone and texted David, excited that he still had some obligation to see me so that I could explain everything.

"You left your laptop at my house," I texted, sending the message the second I had hit the last letter. Sitting back on the couch with his computer on my lap I smiled triumphantly. At least things were looking up a little. The green light on David's computer blinked at me, indicating that even though the screen was closed, the computer was still on.

"That can't be good," I thought aloud, thinking I should probably turn the thing off before giving it back to him. When I opened the screen the same word processor popped up that he'd been typing on after dinner. I glanced at it for a moment, not because I actually intended to read it, but simply because that's where my eyes had fallen. When I read the name "Amelia" on the screen I froze. What could David possibly be writing about me? Was this some sort of digital journal he was keeping?

Now, I don't really consider myself a nosey person. I can keep a secret and I respect people's privacy. But when I saw my name on the computer screen of the boy who I wanted back so badly, I couldn't resist reading on. I had to find out if there was some hint in here as to how I could win him back.

Scrolling to the top of the document I read the title: "The Lonely Girl Syndrome." I stopped reading for a moment. It didn't really sound like a journal entry. And it wasn't exactly formatted to be something turned in to school. At this point I had two different options and I knew how I picked would change things in a big way. I could read on and see exactly what David really thought of me, or I could just close the computer, return it to him, and be grateful that he had taught me so much while we both still trusted each other.

I chose the first option.

Big surprise.

I didn't remember much from what I soon learned was a newspaper article. But some of the phrases stuck in my mind like they'd been burned there. ". . . came from a love-less home to suck the love out of the relationships around her." ". . . withdraws herself from the norms of growing up due to a false sense of superiority." ". . . relies on her looks because nothing resides below the surface."

Each paragraph was worse than the one before it, and I couldn't believe that the person I was reading about was supposed to be me. The details in the article had to come from his year of watching me as he mentioned jobs from ages ago, even jobs I had taken when I went to different schools. Had he followed me to those schools and I just didn't notice? Could he even do that if his parents didn't move like my mom and I did so often?

I was vaguely aware of my phone buzzing next to me but I didn't bother to look down or pick it up. I just stared straight ahead at the screen, too shocked to cry.

I didn't end up reading the whole article. Half was all I could really manage to stomach for the time being. When I had had enough I gently closed the laptop, not bothering to turn it off.

"Okay," I said to the empty room. "This is okay," I said, still more quietly. I didn't seem to be able to really say any-thing that mattered. I could only keep telling myself that everything was okay. This was, of course, pretty far from the truth, but if I kept lying to myself I was hoping I'd eventu-ally start to believe the lie. "Maybe he wasn't adding to the article all this time. Maybe he was . . . deleting it . . . or at least revising it."

One thing I did know was that he had definitely been

doing something to the article since we'd been dating. I just didn't know what.

My phone buzzed next to my leg once more and I finally mustered the sanity to reach down and pick it up. I didn't quite know what to do when I read the words "One Missed Call From David" illuminated across the little screen. Closing that screen my phone revealed to me that I also had a text message from David. I wasn't quite sure if I actually wanted to read it. It would be horrible to read him trying to make up some excuse as to why he'd written the article. Although it would be worse if he didn't . . . if he just asked for his computer back so that he could finally turn in his big story.

Opening up his message didn't really reveal much to me. All he had written was "Is the laptop still on?" I couldn't tell if he was worried, resigned, or just relieved that he wouldn't have to pretend to be interested in me anymore. Sitting there with my phone in my hand I felt so small. The hurt that was bubbling up inside of me felt like more than I could bear, but then the idea that this hurt was caused by a high school relationship made me feel like a fool. I had become exactly like the people I had always made fun of. Maybe David was right. Maybe I did withdraw myself from growing up because I had a false sense of superiority. I had always thought of myself as separate from all of the other students. Like I was part of their world but was above sharing their experiences.

I shook my head, trying to clear it of all of the confusion David's article had brought. Taking a deep breath I decided the only thing I could do would be to actually talk to David. Best case, he didn't mean a word of what he was writing. He was just kidding . . . or trying to prove a point. Worst case, we were through. He hated me and was just using me for his stupid newspaper article.

I decided not to consider the second option anymore or I'd just hang up the phone right as he picked up. As the phone rang, I tried to keep myself from shaking. There had to be some logical explanation to all of this. There was no way David didn't feel as connected to me as I did to him.

On the third ring, I heard David pick up.

"Hey," came his familiar voice on the other end of the phone. He sounded just as bad as I felt, I noted with some hope. Perhaps he didn't want things to be over between us either. I kept my fingers crossed as I spoke in a shaky voice.

"Do you think we can talk?" I asked, my heart feeling like it might just stop altogether.

"Not over the phone," he said after a sizeable pause. "Can you meet me at the park off Hendrix?" he asked.

"Yeah, I'll be there in five minutes," I said, probably a bit too anxiously.

"All right . . . bye." I was glad that at least David still remembered how to end a conversation, though I hoped that was the only context in which I'd ever hear him utter the word "good-bye." Maybe the fact that he felt bad meant that the article wasn't real. Maybe I'd imagined the whole thing.

Or maybe I was just delusional and trying to make myself feel better.

I sped down the street to the park much faster than I should have, happy that I had just taken so much time to make myself look presentable. I pulled into the mostly empty parking lot and instantly spotted David's old blue car. I pulled up beside it, but he wasn't inside. My heart sank for a moment, before I realized that he was probably in the park somewhere. I left the laptop on the passenger side seat, hoping that even if he just wanted to take his computer and go, I could lock the door until we resolved this whole thing.

I walked through the wet grass until I found him sitting on a swing in the abandoned playground.

He looked up when I approached but said nothing, just like he'd done on Friday. At least today he didn't look like he wanted to kill anyone. Instead, he just looked sad and resigned—exactly how I felt.

"You look nice," he said after I sat on the swing beside his.

"Thanks," I answered. I looked over at him and noted that his eyes were red, though I couldn't be sure if it was from lack of sleep or crying. I found myself hoping that either one of these causes was not due to the demise of our relationship.

"So you said you wanted to talk?" he asked carefully, and immediately we had gotten to the hard part. I nodded, not sure exactly where to start or how I could justify my actions to him. Now that I had read the article I almost felt like my little fall off the wagon would be the easy part of the conversation. I decided I'd wait until he brought that situation up. Although from the way he kept looking at me like I was a bomb about to go off, he wasn't quite sure if I had read the article or not. I sighed heavily, figuring I'd kick off this little heart-to-heart with my lies. We could always move to his later.

"I know I promised you I was going to stop all of this but . . . this was something I just had to do." I looked at him, hoping that I could read his reaction and go from there, but his face was completely blank. "I shouldn't have lied to you. Trust is really important to me and it was a stupid mistake . . . I just . . . I didn't know what else to do and at the time it seemed like the only option." I was beginning to ramble desperately. I felt like if I stopped talking for a minute, he would drop the axe on our relationship. Now that I'd confessed to myself that I loved him, it seemed like being without him would be like being without air. The short period of time we'd spent apart had been complete torture. Although for all I knew, the whole time we'd been together had just been a lie to try to get a story out of me. Why couldn't we have a normal relationship?

He looked up at me now, and I was angry with myself for crying in front of him. It was a low trick women used, but I couldn't help myself. The tears wouldn't stop coming now that they'd started. David looked slightly startled that I was crying and I saw a flash of pain flutter across his face. It was a look that made me unhappy but gave me hope at the same time.

"Please don't leave me," I said desperately, and I was fully aware that I'd turned into exactly what I'd wanted to avoid all along. I had become a slave to my emotions, but somehow it wasn't as terrible as I had always expected it to be. "Even being without you for these past two days has been hell." I was babbling again, but I couldn't seem to keep my thoughts in my head. They all wanted to pour out of my mouth at the same time. I just wished he would actually say something. We sat in silence for a few minutes the only sounds audible were those of the crickets and my occasional sniffing as my tears wreaked havoc on the makeup I'd been so proud of moments earlier.

"Did you mean what you said on the phone?" he asked finally, keeping his tone even and looking me squarely in the eyes. I looked at him questioningly. "You love me?" he asked.

I exhaled deeply, the tears making my breath shaky, and nodded my head. I didn't even care if he'd been lying to me. Even if he didn't feel the same way about me, I still felt that way for him and I wouldn't deny it any longer. We sat there in silence for a moment, just staring at each other.

David seemed to be experiencing some internal struggle,

and I was worried about what the conclusion of that struggle would be. "Well, I love you too," he said finally.

I held my breath for a moment. Hoping he would be the one to bring up the article. He said he loved me but would that change if he knew I'd read his secret? Was he only saying it to keep the game up or was he like me: in love but caught in a situation that looked worse than it actually was?

"I just don't understand why you felt you had to keep it a secret from me," he began, though I wasn't quite sure if he was talking about the job I'd taken, or the fact that I knew what he was up to. "I obviously can't stop you from doing whatever you want to do, but a little trust would have been nice, Amelia. I thought we had become an important part of each other's lives. The more complete part. I don't understand why you have this need to keep doing what you did before."

"I wasn't sure you'd get it," I said weakly, now positive he'd been talking about my job . . . not his. "I didn't want to run the risk of having you tell me I couldn't do it." I knew it was a poor explanation as to why I had behaved the way I had, but it was all I could give him.

"That's what trust is all about. You have to trust that I'll be reasonable, and I have to trust that you know what's best for you. I *am* trying." He stood now and for a moment I thought he was going to walk away again. Instead he just paced back and forth, a look of confusion clouding his face.

"I had no intention of leaving you. I just had to take some time to think things over. Like it or not, you're stuck with me now," he said with a small smile. The sadness I had seen in his eyes when I walked up was now gone, and I actually dared to let myself hope that none of this was an act. Maybe the whole thing really did just seem worse than it actually was and there was a simple explanation for it.

"Why, if you don't mind my asking, do you feel that you absolutely need to do this job?" It was quite a reasonable question, I thought, and it struck me as odd that I hadn't mentioned the payment I'd be receiving yet.

"The girl offered me a thousand dollars," I said simply. The look on David's face was so stunned that I wished I had a camera with me to capture the moment forever.

"Are you serious?" he asked incredulously.

"It's Rachel McKlintock," I explained, knowing that name would clear everything up. David was silent for a moment, considering the information I'd just given him. A small, wicked grin crept onto his face and I couldn't even begin to imagine what he was thinking.

"I'm going to sell out . . . just a little," he began.

"You mean you might actually approve of my heathen business now?" I said in mock shock.

"Here's the thing," he said as he sat down on the swing next to me again. "I figure that people like Rachel McKlintock have everything handed to them in life. No matter what difference we try to make, she'll always be able to buy her way out of things, so we're really not doing her a disservice by doing this job."

"We?" I asked inquiringly. David never liked to talk about my business and suddenly he was referring to it as a "we"?

"Or just you . . . either way, she's not going to stop being a snob just because we—I mean you—refuse to help her, so you might as well take advantage of it and make some money while you do it." I couldn't believe all of this was actually coming from David, but I definitely wasn't complaining. There was a nagging feeling in my brain, telling me that he might just be fueling his story, but I tried desperately to ignore it.

"So are you saying there's a loophole to the whole no-breaking-people-up-anymore-ever rule?" I asked skeptically.

"I'm saying that in cases such as these, where the person is really hopeless, you're only doing a disservice to yourself by not accepting the business offer." His wicked grin was still in place, and I knew he just loved the idea of taking money from someone who delighted in throwing it away so freely. "In fact," he went on, "if you want, I'll help you out . . . not that you need it, but it seemed to work out nicely last time."

"What last time are you referring to?" I asked, not quite on the same page as David.

"With Blane. You do whatever it is that you do, and I sweep in as the long-lost boyfriend so that you don't have to worry about getting rid of the boy afterward. It's perfect!" His enthusiasm made me smile, and I couldn't deny that it sounded like a pretty good idea.

"And you'd really be willing to help me out?" I asked doubtfully.

"Like I said, there's nothing morally wrong with it if the person we're doing it for is already socially crippled for life. We're not going to cure the world of rich spoiled kids by refusing them service."

I laughed at this justification but still couldn't believe that he had changed his mind so suddenly. "Well, if we're doing this together, are you free to sweep in on Tuesday? I'll try my best to end it on Monday at dinner, but if he tries to stick around after he and Rachel are through you'll have to work your magic."

"Or we can just assume I'll be working my magic on Tuesday. After all, you want to really show this guy that you aren't available after you've finished the job, that way you don't run the risk of bumping into him later," David said, obviously having thought this through in the short time he had changed his mind about my business.

"Deal," I said simply.

We spent the rest of the night talking about how we could hone our plan to perfection and at least get Alex and Rachel broken up by Monday night. I explained the basics of what I did to David and made sure he had a clear understanding of exactly how this would all work out. By the time we parted in the parking lot that night, I had almost forgotten about the unflattering biography David had written about me. It wasn't until he walked me to my car and noticed the laptop on the front seat that our happy reunion turned somber once more.

"Oh," he said simply, seeing the laptop waiting for him to take it back and continue his exposé. "Where was it?" he asked, nodding toward the computer. He looked almost as if he was afraid to touch it, like it would burn him if he tried to take it back.

"Under the couch. You left it there after you made me dinner." I tried to keep my voice neutral, not wanting to ruin our newly stabilized relationship. Although if he really was just after a story, the stability of our relationship was pretty much gone.

David sighed deeply and ran his fingers through his hair. I loved it when he did that.

"All right, well . . . I don't know if you read what I was writing or not . . . but it doesn't matter . . . because I should just come clean either way."

"I read it," I said in a voice barely above a whisper. I was focused on him so intently that I had been holding my breath. The next few words that came out of his mouth were going to define what our relationship would become.

"All of it?" he asked, his brow furrowed as if he were

confused. I looked down for a moment, I was a little ashamed that I had read his article without asking . . . but he should probably be the one who was more embarrassed in this situation, considering what he had written.

"About half . . . After hearing what you had to say about me . . . Let's just say I didn't really need to read the whole thing." I looked back up to him and the expression he wore surprised me. He didn't look angry or relieved. Instead he just looked sad. I couldn't quite understand where his sadness came in to play but as he came over to me and hugged me, I felt tears welling up in my already red, puffy eyes. This was it. He was leaving me.

"I'm so sorry," he said into my neck. I exhaled deeply. I knew this moment was coming eventually, but that didn't mean I was any more ready for it. "This must have been so hard for you this whole time tonight," he said finally. I nodded silently, still hugging him tightly. I didn't care that he was breaking up with me. I just wanted to hold onto him a little longer.

"It's been hard. I was just hoping somewhere in the back of my mind that you would tell me it was a joke . . . or something," I said thickly, my voice wobbly from the tears streaming down my cheeks. "I didn't even want to bring it up because then all the progress we made tonight would be worthless." David pulled me away from him slowly. I dropped my eyes to the ground, not wanting to meet his gaze as he said the final word in our relationship.

"Amelia?" he asked, tilting my head up so that I would meet his eyes. "How are you so frustrating?"

"Seriously?" I asked, a slight anger mixing with my sadness. "You don't think breaking up with me is enough? Now you have to insult me while you do it?" David simply shook his head, frustration lining his beautiful face.

"Amelia, you aren't understanding me. I'm not breaking up with you . . . I mean . . . I'm sure you might want to break up with me after reading the horrible things I wrote about you . . . but I'm not going to be the one to leave tonight." I looked at him quizzically, not quite following what he was trying to tell me.

"What are you talking about?" I asked, wiping the tears away from my face. Now that they were drying, the salt was beginning to sting my cheeks.

"You said you only read half of the article? Judging by your very emotional reaction, you only read the bad things I wrote, back when I was observing you . . . before I actually got to know you." He looked down guiltily. "Not that it excuses the things I said. I was really awful . . . I went on and on about how you judge people based on their appearance when I completely judged you before ever speaking to you." As he spoke I started to feel that same creeping hope come back to me. Maybe things really weren't as bad as they seemed.

"So the second half is nice?" I asked hopefully.

"Well, that's the thing. I was trying to write a story about perception. You know? Like how I felt about you and what you did before meeting you and if that idea changed after finally meeting you. I thought it would make an interesting article to have a before and after point of view . . . just to see if my perception of you changed at all."

"And did it?"

David smiled at me, pulling me close to him once more.

"I don't think I've ever been so wrong about a person before," he said, kissing the top of my head lightly. "And the thing is, I don't even want to turn the article in anymore. I kind of want to keep it just to remind me how wrong I can be sometimes . . . but for some odd reason, I'm really not that intent on destroying you anymore."

"Oh, well, that's good to know," I said with a laugh. "Because it'd be nice to not worry about my boyfriend being a soul-crushing, life-ruining leech."

"I just said I wouldn't turn the story in . . . not that I was changing who I really am," he said sarcastically. I smiled up at him, letting myself feel relaxed for the first time in a few days.

"So are we still on for Tuesday then?" I asked with a grin.

"Let's bring this guy down."

twenty

Monday night came with all the anticipation of a high-risk bank robbery. Rachel was still faking sick and said she hadn't seen Alex since the last time she was in school. I had somehow gotten him to agree to take me out to his and Rachel's favorite restaurant, which I thought was a bit bold of him. This boy was definitely overconfident and needed his ego taken down a few notches.

I decided to go for a classy look for the date and chose a black and white tweed pencil skirt that came up high on my waist with a tucked-in light pink blouse. The cream colored high heels tied the whole thing together and made me look like something straight out of the 1950s. It took quite a bit of convincing to get Alex to just meet me at the restaurant instead of picking me up, but there was no way he'd believe I was as rich and well connected as him if he saw my house. I was hoping I could get there early enough that he wouldn't even see me get out of my car that was clearly not worth millions of dollars. I finally told him there was a lot of construction going on with our house with the new home theatre we were putting in and I didn't want him to have to walk through all the dust and debris. This seemed to work because he then quickly agreed to simply meet me at the restaurant.

Walking into the restaurant that night was a bit jarring. I was sure the hostess would see right past my façade and tell me to get out because they didn't serve my kind there. Luckily when I told her who I was meeting, she made sure I was comfortable at an intimate table for two. Alex arrived right on time and seemed to be surprised that I was already at the restaurant. Apparently he was used to waiting on high-maintenance dates.

"Marie," he said with a charming smile, "you're here early."

"Actually, Alex, I'm here right on time," I replied, giving him a wink and my most inviting smile. I had to try to keep the small talk up for a while since Rachel said she might be a bit late. We had decided that the best way to get this whole thing done would be to bring her parents along with her so that they would see just how "horrible" Alex was and forbid her from seeing him anymore. Sadly this meant the scene that played out here would probably be very dramatic and loud, but I didn't mind too much since I was positive I wouldn't be coming back to this restaurant again any time soon.

I made sure to rest my hand lightly on the table so that Alex could place his hand gently over mine. Our conversation wasn't particularly exciting, but I pretended to hang on his every word, leaning over the small circular table to get closer to him. The waitress had already come around and taken our orders, which worried me since I had expected Rachel and her parents to be there long before that happened.

I was sorely tempted to take out my phone and call her to ask what was taking so long but I knew that would look far too suspicious, not to mention low-class. Instead I let Alex order for me (since I definitely didn't speak French) and continued to lean into him as if everything he said enthralled me.

After forty-five minutes of listening to him ramble on about why the public school system was so beneath him and he liked when people knew their place in society, Rachel and her parents finally arrived. As much as I didn't want a scene, I was desperate to get out of that restaurant so I decided to help things along a little. I snuggled up closer to Alex so that I was practically sitting on his lap and made a small, innocent observation.

"Alex, why is that girl looking over here? She just keeps staring and it's starting to make me uncomfortable. Could you do something about that?" I asked, looking up at him from under my eyelashes.

"Where?" he asked, obviously surprised that I had spoken, since it was the first time since this date started that I had been able to get a word in. As Alex looked around the room, I saw all of the color drain from his face faster than I thought was healthy. After that it didn't take long for the fight to begin. Rachel strode over to the table like a bull on a rampage with her parents in tow behind her. Alex stood up with his arms spread wide as if trying to say that he had no idea how he had ended up at a nice restaurant with a girl who was definitely not his girlfriend. This, however, didn't seem to work because Rachel drew her hand so far back that she almost hit her startled mother and slapped Alex hard enough to quiet the whole restaurant.

Though I knew there would be a scene, I hadn't expected such a forceful reaction, especially since Rachel had planned the whole thing. I thought she would at least cut the boy some slack since she knew he wasn't technically cheating. This knowledge didn't seem to faze her at all.

"Daddy, do you see what I have to put up with?" she shrieked, drawing the attention of everyone who hadn't already been alerted by the slap. "He's disloyal! I've been trying to tell you for so long. I deserve so much better than him, Daddy!" After this proclamation, Rachel broke down into what I can only describe as the most poorly acted fit of crying I had ever seen. Her mother wrapped an understanding arm around her daughter's shaking shoulders, which I found at least slightly endearing. They might be filthy rich and spoiled rotten but they still possessed human emotion, which was more than I expected. The "human emotion" coming from Rachel's father, however, was less endearing and more terrifying.

I couldn't quite understand what he was saying but he was definitely turning an unhealthy shade of scarlet as he bellowed at a still-dumbfounded Alex. I didn't quite know who I should feel sorry for in the situation that was playing out before me; though I was quickly starting to suspect that I shouldn't really feel sorry for any of them. Instead I sat awkwardly at the table, fully aware that many of the eyes were turned on me. I was officially cast as the "other woman" in this scenario. I twisted my cloth napkin into a small pillar in my lap before finally deciding it would be best to just get out of there. My usual apologize and dash strategy didn't seem appropriate for this situation so I had to think quickly.

Standing up I shot an icy death glare at Alex and threw my cloth napkin down on the table. Rachel's father had stopped yelling for a moment, presumably to catch his breath, so I took that opportunity to say in a high-pitched, indignant voice, "I can't believe you didn't tell me you had a girlfriend," before stomping out of the restaurant, hoping I wouldn't trip over anything and draw even more attention to myself.

Once I reached my car, I turned and looked behind me to make sure Alex or Rachel's family wasn't coming out of the restaurant to see my old, unimpressive car. Much to my delight they were nowhere to be found.

I drove home with a grin plastered to my face, excited to recount the night's events to David and discuss our plan of attack for the next day, though I suspected that after that performance, Alex wouldn't find me quite as appealing as he had just moments ago.

I wore a low-cut, teal, silk blouse to school on Tuesday with black skinny jeans and open-toed teal heels. It was easy to spot Alex in his normal spot by the tennis courts. He looked eager as I walked up behind him, which I thought was odd since I had just caused him quite a bit of grief the night before. I had to think of a good excuse as to why I would be coming around after I had declared my loathing so forcefully just a day ago. He glanced around often; apparently looking for someone that I assumed was me. I decided not to disappoint him. Leaning over behind him, I whispered a quick, "Looking for someone?" in his ear. His cheeks instantly turned red when he saw me, though he kept himself beautifully composed.

"Hey, Marie," he said casually, though by the way his eyes kept wandering to my lips, I knew I'd snagged him. "I'm really sorry about last night. I should have told you about that little detail," he said casually. I figured that when he said "little detail" he meant the fact that he had a girl-friend who he was cheating on with me. Instead of showing my true disgust for this boy, who apparently hadn't learned his lesson, I simply shrugged my shoulders.

"I've already forgotten about it," I said sweetly.

I spent all of my energy that morning being as openly flirtatious as I possibly could be without literally throwing myself at Alex. David spent the day away from the spot because, according to him, just because he'd agreed it was a worthy cause, it didn't mean he'd be able to stand by and watch some other guy ogle me. I found his jealousy endearing.

I left school Tuesday afternoon (David and I had agreed not to meet in the parking lot in case Alex showed up) and drove down to the park, slipping out of my heels and exchanging them for the black flip-flops I had tossed in my car that morning. David was waiting for me in his car, and I got in the passenger seat. We had decided that since we weren't able to make our date a few days ago, we would celebrate our inevitable victory tonight by going to dinner. It had been my idea to meet in the parking lot of the park rather than at my house, after our last experience there. David assured me that wasn't likely to happen again but agreed to the park.

We went to the same Italian restaurant he had taken me to on our first "fake" date. The food seemed better this time, and the conversation was infinitely better. We sped through the list of "favorites" (favorite movie, color, animal, food) and worked our way into goals for the future. I had much more to say about my goals, since I didn't posses any favorites of my own. The conversation continued as we migrated back to the park and ended up lying on a blanket in the grass.

David had his arm around me, enabling me to rest my head on his chest as we spoke. The lights around the park made it difficult to see the stars, but I wasn't looking at the sky anyway. With my eyes trained on the perfect boy beside me, I asked him to tell me about his family. I knew it sounded like an oddly masochistic question coming from someone in a broken home, but I actually enjoyed hearing about normal families.

"Well, you already know about my parents. I've got one little sister and no brothers, but I do have a rather amusing grandma," he said, sounding very much like someone telling a bedtime story. "She grew up in the south but moved down to Simi Valley when my dad moved to Thousand Oaks. She always says the most inappropriate things." He laughed softly at some unspoken memory and continued. "Most of the time she's pretty funny, but we have to be careful when we're out in public. Some people don't understand where she's coming from."

I closed my eyes and listened to the steady beat of David's heart, never wanting this moment to end. "What about the rest of your family?" I asked, just wanting to keep him talking. The way he talked about his family was so loving that it made me wish I had that kind of relationship with my own.

"The rest of my family is pretty normal. We try to get together every few years, but it's difficult with everyone spread out all over the country." He shrugged and fell silent, and we both listened to the wind blowing through the trees for a little while. After a few more moments of silence, I voiced a thought that I had been entertaining since our talk a few days earlier.

"David?"

"Mmm?"

"I was just thinking about how well this job is working out . . . and how well Blane worked out, and I was thinking . . . maybe if we did a background check on each client to make sure they weren't some sort of 'chronic dumper,' we could still keep the business going."

He didn't say anything for a minute, and I thought maybe I'd overestimated the appeal of this proposal.

"Go on," he said after a moment, much to my relief.

"Well, maybe you could perform the background check since you have vast journalistic skills," I said as I nudged him with my shoulder. We had moved on from his less-than-kind description of me in his article, but that didn't mean I couldn't taunt him with it every now and then. "Maybe you could decide if the person is a worthy client and I could do what I do, then you could sweep in and save me from any commitment at the last second." I paused, thinking through this a bit more now that I'd said it out loud. "Maybe we could say that everyone can get one breakup before they're no longer eligible for the service. The only time we'd per-form multiple breakups for the same person would be in spe-cial cases like Rachel McKlintock, where they're already so spoiled that our refusal wouldn't make a difference."

I looked up at David and saw that he was actually work-ing through my proposal in his head, which, honestly, was much more than I'd expected. I tried to let him think without staring at him, so I closed my eyes and just concentrated on the way his chest rose and fell with each slow breath he took.

"I like that idea," he said finally, actually sounding pleased. I looked up at him to see him smiling back down at me. He kissed the top of my head and I reveled in the odd compromise to the two futures I had originally imagined. I was the luckiest girl alive to get to have a little of both of the worlds I couldn't seem to give up.

Project "Alex Swensen" was in full swing by the time I pulled into the parking lot on Wednesday morning. David had scoped out the perfect spot where he could keep an eye on what was going on and sweep in at just the right moment. No matter what happened, today was a pivotal moment for this job, and a lot rested on exactly how I played the whole thing.

I emerged from my car in a dark blue lace tank top and a short white skirt. I passed David in the parking lot briefly, but we didn't acknowledge each other's presence, though I could have sworn I heard him say something about how I looked like a sailor. I wanted to turn around and shoot some counter attack about how he had dressed like a rich kid today, but I had to stay focused on the job. I had a very expensive looking, but very fake diamond necklace around my neck, and I had curled my hair once more, letting it fall wildly around my face.

David and I had both gotten to school a bit late that day and therefore had to wait until break to perform the entire scene. It worked out better that way, in my opinion, because having more time was always an advantage. It left room for mistakes. I walked to my class, taking note of the various prom posters around school. They all advertised the same date: May 17. It was only four days from now— this Saturday night. I wondered fleetingly if David would ask me, or if I even wanted him to ask me. Prom seemed like such a trivial ritual, but it would be fun to go. I had never been to a dance before, and while I was sure actually dancing was out of the question, it would be nice to get all dressed up with David.

I spent my entire class texting David to make sure he was ready for everything. He quickly reminded me that it wasn't hard to strut in and act like he loved me. This made me smile and blush deeply, which didn't escape the notice of my teacher. I tried to keep my emotions more at bay for the rest of the class but continued to text David any time my teacher wasn't looking.

By the time I left class and headed toward the tennis courts, I was feeling like a secret agent. I was even considering coming up with my own theme music when a look at Alex brought me back to the here and now. I noticed with some apprehension that his friends weren't flanking him as they normally were. I started to wonder if I had overestimated my charm. Alex wore an odd expression that I couldn't really understand, and I was slowly becoming convinced that he had found out the entire plan and had dismissed his cronies to beat me to a pulp, or something equally as horrible. Knowing him, that "equally as horrible'" thing would have something to do with discontinuing my nonexistent trust fund.

"Marie?" he said as I approached, and I wondered if he was looking for confirmation of my identity or simply a nod to show I was listening. I opted for the nod. "I've been thinking about you a lot these past couple days," he began, and I could almost taste the victory. I even felt a bit bad, since he seemed to possibly care about me.

"Have you?" I said noncommittally.

"Yes . . . and I've been thinking that we could be good for each other. I mean, with my family's connections and your family's connections, we could do anything." Oh, how romantic. He wanted to date me because we could plot to take over the world together. That's what every girl wants out of a relationship.

"Really? Because I was beginning to get the impression that you and Rachel might still be together," I said, wanting him to actually tell me that he had broken up with her.

"Me? No, I'm not with Rachel anymore," he said casually.

"Is that so?" I said simply, assuming with some relief

that this meant he and Rachel were officially broken up. I hadn't been able to actually confirm this fact since Rachel seemed too busy to take my calls all of a sudden. Shaking the thoughts from my mind and turning my focus back to Alex, I smiled, trying not to let him see my distaste for him. I was desperate for David to sweep in and bail me out, but he hadn't come yet and I couldn't quite understand why.

"So, with that out of the way, I was wondering if you would want to be my girlfriend. Just imagine how much influence we'd have. No doors would be locked to us." This boy's method of romancing a girl really wasn't a flowers and chocolates approach, was it? I waited for a moment, trying to look like I was thinking it over, while in reality I was waiting for David to make his big entrance. Suddenly I was beginning to panic, wondering if maybe he thought we were doing it at lunch and was just waiting for me by the library. I looked around nervously, but I couldn't spot him anywhere.

"Your girlfriend?" I repeated, trying to buy myself some time to think.

"Yeah. I really do think it's a good match, and I'm sure our parents would agree."

"Well, there's no denying that," I said enthusiastically, still waiting for David to rescue me from the clutches of Stock Exchange Boy.

"So, what do you say?" he asked, obviously a bit put-off by the fact that I hadn't answered him in the affirmative right away.

"I say . . . um . . . that's a really generous offer . . ." I trailed off, not quite sure where to go from there.

"But one she sadly can't accept," said the sandy blond–haired boy who had suddenly appeared right beside me. I didn't have to fake my relief at the sight of him, though I wanted to stomp on his foot for taking so long.

"Jackson, what on earth are you doing here?" I asked, my face the epitome of astonishment. "I thought your parents took you on holiday to . . . to . . . Paris." I had forgotten my line, apparently, but I thought my recovery was convincing enough.

"I told them to fly me back early when I realized I was going to miss your birthday, honey bear." I had to choke back a laugh at David's moment of improv. We had definitely not decided on disgusting pet names, though I wouldn't mind giving him a taste of his own medicine.

"Well, I'm so glad you did, snuggle bunny," I said in the most pathetic baby voice I could manage. Alex looked as if he wanted to vomit, which I couldn't blame him for. If I thought someone was seriously calling her significant other snuggle bunny, I'd have to run for a trash can too. David looked as if he wouldn't last much longer. His stomach was shaking with the effort of holding his laughter in. "Sorry, Alex, I didn't know I was sending that kind of signal to you. But I swear, it's not you, it's me . . ." I shrugged innocently and took David's hand.

"Let's go make birthday preparations on my yacht," David added enthusiastically, making it difficult for me to keep my expression neutral. "It was lovely to meet you, Andre," he said over his shoulder as we left. If David hadn't done a relatively thorough background check to show me that, until Rachel, who was even more well-connected than him, Alex had been quite the player, I would have felt slightly bad about the whole thing.

"Honey bear?" I asked, as we walked down the hallway to the now familiar spot by the library. David laughed loudly at his own cleverness and messed his hair up, loosening the gel that had kept it slicked back for our little show.

"Honey bear is nothing compared to snuggle bunny.

Where did you even get that from?" he asked incredulously.

"Just by looking at you, lovekins," I said, pinching his cheek as we stood at our spot. Sitting was out of the question in my short skirt.

"All things considered, I think that went pretty well," he told me, after disheveling his hair to his satisfaction.

"It would have gone better if you had actually come in when you were supposed to," I said accusingly. "What took you so long?"

"It was fun to watch you sweat," he said cheekily. I hit him on the arm and pretended to pout for as long as I could stand it, which was only a few seconds.

"Well, say you're sorry so I can forgive you or no yacht ride for you."

"I'm so sorry, Amelia Marie Bedford. From now on I will ruin the lives of others right on schedule." I gave him a sharp look but ignored his apology and pulled out my phone.

"Now, to see if everything worked out with Rachel," I said, by way of an explanation.

"Hello?" came Rachel's sleepy voice. I just couldn't understand how that girl could sleep in so late all the time.

"Hey Rachel, it's Amelia. I was just wondering if everything worked out all right? Because if it didn't, then you have a cheating boyfriend on your hands."

"Oh yeah, Daddy was really upset and said I couldn't date him for another minute," she said nonchalantly. I suppose it would have been too much trouble for her to call and tell me this herself. "So I'll send someone over to the school to slip the money into your locker next week. I'm taking a small vacation from the whole public school thing."

"All right, well, good luck with that," I said insincerely as I hung up the phone. David looked at me inquiringly and I just said, "Rich people."

"Rich people indeed," he agreed as he looked me up and down. "I wasn't aware that rich people dressed like sailors," he said with a laugh.

"At least I didn't wear something straight out of a cologne ad," I said incredulously, though my voice still held a humorous edge.

"Hey, you just said wear 'expensive looking clothes.' Slacks and a button-up shirt are expensive," he said reasonably. "Although maybe popping the collar was a bit much." I just shook my head at his logic, a smile creeping onto my face. "Besides," he continued, "I wanted to look nice when I asked you." I stared at him, waiting for him to finish his sentence, but apparently that was all I was getting without giving him a little prodding.

"Ask me what?"

"If you would be interested in going to prom with me." He looked at me expectantly now, all joking gone from his face. My smile widened for a moment before melting away.

"I think all of the tickets are sold out," I answered dismally.

"Yeah, I figured that would happen . . . that's why I bought them when we decided to call a truce last week." I could tell that he was pretty pleased with himself, and quite frankly, I was too.

"I would love to," I said happily, trying not to look like a grinning idiot. David beamed at me before his face became serious once more. "Oh no. There's more?" I asked, completely at a loss for what else he could possibly need to say.

"I know it's none of my business but I figured . . . maybe getting a dress and everything would be a good opportunity for you to spend some time with your mom." His voice was barely above a whisper, but I heard him perfectly.

It had been sweet of him to think of that, but I couldn't

imagine my mom and me spending a girl's day out to go shopping for a dress. Not wanting to spoil his plans, though, I said, "Yeah, maybe," without much hope that my mom would agree to come with me.

"Just promise you'll ask?" he said hopefully.

"I promise."

twenty-one

My mom wasn't home when I got back from school that day but, wanting to be true to my promise, I left her a note telling her David had asked me to prom and that I would like her to come dress shopping with me if she had the chance. I wondered if she would even come home before Saturday to get the note. Even if she didn't, it was none of my concern because I had upheld my part of the bargain and I was going dress shopping tomorrow night, with or without her.

To say that I was feeling slightly less than happy with my mother would be an understatement. I couldn't seem to figure out what bothered me most about her choice: the fact that it was so horribly wrong or the fact that she felt the need to cut me out of her life to live one that she thought was more exciting. If it weren't for David holding my hand through the past few days, I wouldn't have known how to cope with everything.

With my note taped to the refrigerator and my home-work all finished, I decided to paint for a while. I kept my phone beside the easel in case David called and dove into painting something very green—something the same color as his eyes. Only minutes into the painting, my phone began to vibrate, instantly catching my attention. I wiped the paint off of my hands hastily and picked up the phone only to see an unfamiliar number on the screen. I hesitantly flipped the phone open to see who my mysterious caller was.

"Hello?" I asked cautiously. No one ever called me, since no one really had my number.

"Amelia?" It was a voice I knew I recognized but couldn't quite place a face with.

"Yes?" I answered, trying to sound politely confused.

"It's Nate." So that's where I'd heard the voice before. Nate sounded slightly distressed, and I couldn't understand why he'd be calling me unless something had happened to Karen.

"Is she all right?" I asked instantly, finding that I actually cared about the girl's well-being.

"I guess so," he answered without much enthusiasm. "I wouldn't really know. I haven't seen her since the last time I talked to you."

"What?" I asked astonished. I knew her mom had given in pretty easily, but I hadn't expected her to go back on her word. I figured that she would just be a bit more strict than she had let on.

"She never lets me see her . . . but it's hard to exactly say she's keeping her from me, because every time I want to come over, she has a really good excuse." Nate sounded weary, as if his constant efforts to see Karen had worn him out. "First it was a doctor's appointment, then she wasn't feeling well enough to have any company, now she's saying that Karen needs her rest to regain her strength . . . I mean, maybe this is all true, but it's just so convenient that this all happens every time I try to see her."

I closed my eyes, trying to think of some way to help the situation. "Have you asked her mom about this? Confronted her to see if she really is lying?"

"No . . . I don't want to sound too pushy. After all, Karen really could be feeling sick, and I don't want to make it worse by forcing her to see me."

"Well, have you tried talking to Karen?" I suggested, though I was sure he had definitely tried that.

"She won't answer her phone," he said with a sigh. I mulled this over for a moment, trying to think of some way around this.

"Nate, you're just going to have to be the grown-up here. You need to tell her mom that you want to see Karen and call her out on this. Ask her if she's lying to you. It may seem a bit direct, but if you don't do it now, her mom will just keep phasing you out until you've lost interest." I wasn't really sure I was giving him sound advice, but it was the best solution I could see to the problem.

"I think she'll let me see her eventually. I think she's just trying to keep me away until after prom . . . she thinks it'll be too much for Karen to handle."

I sighed, seeing his point. "Just try what I told you and I'll try to think of a better solution in the meantime," I said reassuringly, feeling a bit like Dear Abby.

"All right," he answered, sounding like he didn't have much faith in my solution. "Thanks again, Amelia."

After I got off the phone with him, I couldn't help but feel like this was largely my fault. After all, I had been the one who suggested they talk to her mother in the first place. And now Nate didn't see Karen at school or at home. He just didn't see her at all. And it was because I had given them the alternative of having her go back to being homeschooled. It was another brilliant idea from Amelia Marie Bedford.

❋

Thursday the 15th arrived with as much gusto as a Thursday could muster. It was one day closer to Saturday, which made me feel a bit more excited about the coming prospect of actually going to prom. At first I hadn't been amazingly excited about the whole thing, but the fact that I'd actually get to participate in a normal human experience was something I was greatly looking forward to.

I went downstairs after pulling on what I figured would be my normal wardrobe from then on. My jeans and colored tank tops perfectly suited my personality—the real me that it had taken so long to find—unassuming but well adapted. I smiled at my own comparison and pulled an apple out of the fridge. As I closed the heavy white door I glanced at my note to see if it had moved at all, only to find a new piece of paper stuck to the fridge with the simple words "I'd like that" scribbled in blue pen.

I stared at the note for a while, trying to determine if I was just really sleepy, or if my mom had actually said she'd like to spend time with me. I turned this over in my mind as I made my way to school that day. It felt almost surreal as I pulled into the parking lot. Today was the first day of my new life. David and I had reached an understanding that we could both live with: I had made a human connection so utterly and deeply significant to me that I might actually make it out of high school with some sanity, and I was coming to school today without the burden of other people's problems on my shoulders. Granted, I was worried about what would happen with Nate and Karen, but the situation was entirely out of my hands. All I could do for them was attempt to keep dispensing sound advice.

I met David in the parking lot, and his warm smile was not lost on me. It was as if he too could see the future stretching out before us, full of the unknown and the exciting prospects that youth offers. I slipped my hand into his as we walked into the busy school, talking quietly about the various trivial plans that prom entailed: what color would my dress be, could he get his tie to match, what time he should pick me up. As much as I'd always made fun of other people for wasting their breath talking about those kinds of things, it felt nice to worry about something so unimportant. My decision on what color dress I would wear to prom probably wouldn't affect the rest of my life, so it was a decision I was willing to make without much thought.

The day passed quickly and uneventfully, which made me happier than any excitement-filled day could have. I said good-bye to David in the parking lot and drove home, wondering if my mom would really be there waiting for me. There was no black car parked across the street when I pulled up, so at least I was safe on that account.

As I walked through the door, I dropped my black backpack on the carpet, peering into rooms as I made my way toward the kitchen. I found her there, sitting at the table with her head in her hands. She instantly brightened when I walked into the room, even if her smile was less than heartfelt.

"You're going to prom," she said with all the pride of a mother who'd finally married off her spinster daughter.

"Yep," I said awkwardly. Though I felt that people were just instinctively good at things that should come naturally, like kissing and spending time with their families, my mother and I seemed to lack that natural ability to make small talk with one another. We got into her white SUV and drove through the winding roads of Thousand Oaks to the mall where my future prom dress was hiding. We didn't say much in the car on the way there, though she made a comment about an old song on the radio, saying that she could remember listening to it as a teenager.

The mall was relatively crowded for a Thursday, though I attributed that to the upcoming prom. Teenagers roamed the tile walkways in groups, and most of them, I noticed, were not with their mothers. Then again, when had I ever done things the way everyone else did them? We searched through a few of the big department stores, thumbing through racks of hot pink silk before my mom finally asked what should have been an obvious question.

"What kind of dress are you looking for, Amelia?" She always liked to use my name when she spoke to me. When I was younger she told me that she had loved the name Amelia and had wanted to change her name when she was little. I figured that's why she always used it whenever she could. She loved the sound of it.

"I'm not sure," I said honestly. It was rare for someone to ask me what I wanted, and even more rare for me to think about my own personal preference. After years of being a clone of whoever I worked for, it was difficult for me to determine what I, myself, actually liked and disliked.

"Well, what color do you want?" she asked, examining a pale blue dress. I thought of David's eyes for a moment and seriously considered saying green, but I quickly decided against it, knowing the color would wash me out. I thought about colors that had appealed to me when looking through magazines, and things I'd seen in my everyday life that had caught my eye. The only thing I could think of was a word and not a color. Unassuming. That was what I wanted. And once the word came to me, the color did too, something that could be appropriately elegant while still remaining unassuming.

"I want a champagne colored dress," I said finally. My mom looked at me skeptically for a moment.

"That's not exactly a popular color, Amelia," she informed

me, and as I looked around at the racks of dresses, I could see that she was right. The closest thing this store offered was a sort of off-white or pale yellow. Not quite champagne. We looked through a few more big department stores before finding a store that carried only prom dresses. Surely this store had to hold the dress I was looking for. Browsing through the racks for only a few minutes, I found it. I found my size and put it on in the dressing room, examining myself in the mirror.

It was a floor-length silk gown that hugged my curves nicely. It had thick straps that crisscrossed in the back, and a sweetheart neckline. It was perfect, and it was champagne.

The grand total came to $300, which I paid myself, much to my mother's protests. As a compromise she insisted that I let her buy the champagne heels to match. And with our purchases made, we were on our way home, our little mother-daughter bonding experience at an end. As we were stopped at a particularly long red light, however, my mother unexpectedly said, "I'm not a bad person, you know." Caught completely off-guard, I wasn't quite sure how to respond to that. I hadn't accused her of being a bad person—I'd just bought my prom dress and minded my own business. "I make bad decisions sometimes, but parents are people too, Amelia."

I had no idea where this was coming from, but I decided it was something she needed to get out, so I simply said, "I know," afraid that any other response would spark the wrong reaction.

"I don't want you thinking I'm a bad person. Some people just deal with heartache differently." Now I was starting to feel I knew what she was talking about, but I still couldn't be sure.

"You mean Dad?" I asked as innocently as I could. I looked at her out of the corner of my eye, my mother whom

I'd never really had a relationship with. Her short, dark brown hair was cut in a bob, and her nails were always perfectly manicured. She was always well put together, never showing any vulnerability to me or anyone else. And here she was, crying in the driver seat of her white SUV. Not overly dramatic, heartrending sobs, but just a few, silent tears that she quickly wiped away.

"Sometimes when you face rejection it leaves you changed, and no one can bring you back to where you used to be, but that doesn't mean you should stop trying," she said cryptically. And that was the end of our conversation. She didn't say another word, and I didn't try to coax anything else out of her. I wasn't exactly sure what I would say if I did speak. We murmured the appropriate "that was fun" and "let's do that again sometime" phrases that are polite after such an outing and then went our separate ways, back to interacting through post-it notes again. At least for a while.

twenty-two

Saturday came faster than I expected it to, and I was shocked when I woke up on the morning of prom, completely excited for my first real high school interaction. I got my hair done that morning at a salon, where they pulled it up and twisted it back into an elegant knot on the back of my head. I had decided to stay blonde for prom since I hadn't really decided on a hair color I liked just for myself yet. David told me he didn't have a preference either way, and I was glad he wasn't one of those boys who thought any girl, no matter how dumb or how unattractive, was instantly "hot" because she was blonde.

By the time David picked me up that evening, I was feeling the butterflies that I was sure were customary for these types of situations. My mom had stuck around long enough to take pictures of David and me together before leaving to wherever it was she went.

"You look amazing," David said, giving me a smile that could melt butter.

"You don't look too bad yourself," I replied as I beamed at him. We hadn't bothered matching his tie to my dress since I didn't know the color of my dress until a few days before prom. Instead he wore a nice black suit with a black skinny tie. The old fashioned look suited him perfectly.

"I have something for you," he said suddenly before we walked out the door. I raised an eyebrow at him inquiringly and he pulled out a little velvet box. "Remember how I told you my mom makes jewelry?" I nodded, urging him to continue. "Well, I asked her for some lessons and I . . . I made you a bracelet. It's not as amazing as the stuff she makes, but I thought you might like it."

Feeling overcome with the love I felt for this boy, I opened the box he had handed to me to find a small pink gold bracelet covered in champagne-colored stones. "It's amazing," I said honestly as he secured it around my wrist.

"I thought following tradition has never really been our style, so instead of a corsage, this would do nicely." Entwining my hand with his, I gave him one long kiss that was interrupted by a knock on the door. David and I exchanged confused looks, but I answered the door since there really wasn't much other choice, unless we wanted to spend prom night locked in my house . . . but we wouldn't get into that possibility at the moment.

As the door swung open, I saw Nate standing on my front porch. He was wearing a suit much like the one David had on and looked as if he'd been crying for hours. His rosy cheeks were especially red today and they matched his bloodshot eyes.

"Nate, what's wrong?" I asked urgently. David was by my side.

"I finally got Karen's mom to really talk to me," he said, between sharp intakes of breath, "I guess she's really not doing so well." I had never seen a boy cry—which was saying something since I was in the breakup business—and the scene before me truly broke my heart.

"What did she say exactly?" I urged, hoping to get more information out of him to help me assess the situation.

"I told her that I was on my way to pick Karen up for the prom whether she wanted me to or not, and she told me that Karen was too weak to even get out of bed. Her mom's really worried about her." A few tears ran down Nate's rosy cheeks, and I looked at David for a moment as we silently exchanged an understanding between us.

"Nate, can you take us to Karen's house?" I asked. David and I were both perfectly healthy at the moment, and I knew Nate would never compromise Karen's health, so there didn't seem to be too much harm in our visiting her. "If she can't go to the prom, we'll just have to take the prom to her," I said resolutely.

Nate brightened slightly at this suggestion, and he jumped into his green car, with David and I close behind, and drove to Karen's house.

It took some convincing to get Karen's mom to let us in to see her, but in the end I think she was happy that her daughter wouldn't be left out of the festivities of the evening. As the night wore on and the four of us began to talk about our plans for the future, plans Karen might not ever get to live out, I wondered if maybe we all just wanted to belong somehow. Maybe the reason I had been so scared of sinking to the level of everyone else my whole life was because somewhere, in the back of my mind, I feared that I wouldn't measure up. Maybe I worried that the experiences I thought I should have in high school wouldn't measure up to my own expectations.

Though it should have been a sad occasion to see Karen lying in her bed, looking pale and weak as we talked about the trip we would all take this summer, just because we could, it was a happy moment. Karen laughed feebly as Nate held her hand, and I was immensely grateful for all of the things I had always taken for granted—the future I had always assumed everyone was entitled to.

In the end, I had come to terms with myself and what my life was. It wasn't particularly bad or good. And as my mom tried to say, even with her poor communication skills, the individual journey of our lives doesn't really label us bad or good. Life was whatever I chose to make of it.

And though I traded in what I thought was an important high school experience, almost pivotal to my feeling that human connection, what I gained was so much more than I could have ever imagined. Something much richer.

I discovered love.

discussion questions

1. Throughout the book we're given information by Amelia, our narrator. She seems to tell the audience and those she interacts with about the unique bond she has with her mother. When we discover the truth about the disconnected and almost nonexistent relationship between her and her mother, we start to find that our narrator is not wholly reliable. Why does Amelia feel the need to stretch the truth about her relationship with her mother? What other half-truths does Amelia give the reader that we soon see the reality behind?

2. Amelia makes a point of stating over and over again that she does not participate in normal high school life because she does not want to be reduced to a simple stereotype. If this fate is so loathsome to her, why does she categorize her clients based on their clothes, music, and friends? Does this mean she thinks less of the people who hire her? Does her perception of others change as the story progresses?

3. When Amelia is breaking up Rachel McKlintock and Alex Swensen, she can't help but notice that Rachel's mother comforts her daughter in her time of need. How

do you think this affects Amelia emotionally? What contrasts can you see between Amelia's mother and Rachel's?

4. Throughout the story David talks with Amelia about his family and how close he is to them. We never see David's family in the story, and Amelia is never introduced to them. Unlike the often unreliable descriptions of reality we get from Amelia, should we assume David is telling the truth about his perfect family? Why do you think Amelia is never introduced to them?

5. Amelia has spent her entire high school career thus far trying to remain anonymous and only interact with people when her job calls for it. She makes no human connections until David comes along and sacrifices a normal high school experience for something she originally felt was better. Do you think Amelia regrets the ultimate consequences of her seclusion? When do you think she starts to admit to herself that living separate from the high school experience may not have been the best choice?

6. When Amelia first learns why Karen and Nate can't be together, she imagines a "Romeo and Juliet" scenario. Is this another instance of Amelia categorizing people or is this somehow different? What differences do you see between this form of categorization and her typical jock, nerd, and punk categorizations?

about the author

Shannen Crane Camp was born and raised in Southern California where she developed a love of reading and writing, completing her first (very) short story in the fifth grade. She continued to write throughout junior high and high school before finally deciding that enough was enough; it was time to be an author. She moved to Provo, Utah, to attend Brigham Young University where she attained a bachelor's degree in Media Arts and a very well received proposal from her fellow California resident Josh Camp. The two are now happily married and living in Provo.

The Breakup Artist is Shannen's first published novel. Feel free to contact her at Shannencbooks@hotmail.com or visit her blog at http://shannencbooks.blogspot.com.